The Angel Paradigm

Michelle Preno

ISBN-13: 978-0-9863143-5-3

Dedicated to my brother, my sister-in-law, and my niece.
I hope to see more of you (and everyone else) soon.

0. Michelle Preno, Author - - Preface

"If men were angels, no government would be necessary."

While the words of James Madison may be applied as something of an analogy, they do not cover the scope of the Angel Paradigm—not in the slightest. The depth of this concept goes well beyond the institution of government and spreads through the multifaceted layers of culture and society around the globe.

In fact, the Paradigm's very omnipresence causes the true meaning to be both elusive and evolving. While there are no serious errors within the common understanding, there is also no depth. Have we reached it, will we reach it, or does it even matter—these and other questions are the doors to lengthy philosophical discussion, much of which will be repeated throughout this narrative.

Of course, none of these questions will ever find an outright answer, but that's not the point. The point is to understand the Paradigm from all angles possible because like it or not, it is at the forefront of the future of the human race. And that is precisely where this book comes in.

The origin of the Paradigm cannot be pinpointed to an exact moment, but it certainly existed before the Robotic Revolution. However it wasn't until after the Revolution—in the time leading up to the Initiative—that the Paradigm became an international cultural phenomenon. Now that we have passed the Initiative, it's time to take a look at these questions once more, to deepen our understanding and help plot what comes next.

The collection of accounts within these pages provides a multifaceted and functional description of the Angel Paradigm. Over the course of several years, I have had the unique privilege of meeting and interviewing many of the key players in both the Robotic Revolution and the Earth Initiative. I have taken these conversations, interspersed with other references, and attempted to create a fluid and informative narrative of sorts.

Without a doubt, the backbone of this narrative is the story of Michael Trualt. In fact, this project began as an interview with Dr. Jeffery Thompson, current Chair of the Robotics Committee of the Earth Legislature, on the subject of Michael Trualt from the perspective of a colleague. The man's influence on the Paradigm arguably surpasses any other individual, but his story has become almost as elusive and evolving as the Paradigm itself, taking a life of its own from the media and the public.

In these pages, I make no attempt to portray his actions as good or bad, though most of those interviewed in this book have included their own view of the matter. I also hope to remind my audience not to narrow their perception; despite his overwhelming influence, Trualt and his actions were and are just one man's view of the Paradigm. It would be a mistake to associate the concept solely with him.

Most of these accounts were compiled in the last three years, and I have provided ample citation of the process for added transparency. Each contributor was asked to approve the final form of their contribution before it would appear in this collection (except one, where this was impossible). It is my hope that this book will shed new light on the Angel Paradigm and perhaps help humanity understand the future that lies ahead.

Men will never be angels, but maybe robots will.

1. Jeffery Thompson, Roboticist - - Edited Interview[1]

Dr. Thompson is widely considered one of the top roboticists in the world and has been honored with the Turing Award for his contributions to the development of the first cerebral unit. His expertise has made him the first Chair of the Robotics Committee of the new Earth Legislature, but his Senatorial duties come second to his scientific pursuits. He is currently working on the independent morality problem as an Affiliated Researcher of United Robotics's central processing department.

You know, this question—about the Paradigm—it comes up almost every day in my work. I'm sure you've taken a look at some of my other statements regarding the matter, but I wonder if you would notice a trend—a sort of evolution? My views have definitely changed over the years, and I can't say they won't be different tomorrow, and a lot of that has to do with the independent morality problem.[2]

But let's take a step back for a moment. Before I talk about any personal experience, I should underline some postulates. First, for the purposes of this narrative, I will assume we are talking about robots as humanoid mechanical agents of advanced general intelligence. I will also omit biorobotics in most of its current forms. This is admittedly a major omission, particularly because biorobotics may determine the fate of the Angel Paradigm as we know it, but I am simply not qualified to discuss the subject at length.

With these postulates in mind, I will start by saying that in my opinion, there are two main components of the classic Angel Paradigm: servitude and supervision. Before the Revolution, and through its early years, the

---

[1] Conducted face-to-face 22-23.07.2131. Current form approved by Dr. Thompson 04.01.2134.

[2] The independent morality problem refers to the study and attempted implementation of independent morality in robots. Currently, robot morality can be programmed for simple cases, but it is dependent on an outside determination of right or wrong, as well as minimal variation in the case structure.

Paradigm was realistically limited to servitude: robots would serve us to the point where we wouldn't have to worry about anything, we could just do whatever made us happy. Most of us can agree even now that future hasn't truly arrived, but to be fair, we've made a good deal of progress in that direction.

What I find far more important and fascinating is how the Paradigm changed with the Initiative: namely, how the supervision aspect came into play. But we will save that for later. For now, I will focus on what I saw of the Paradigm in the days of the Revolution, starting from the beginning.

I was 8 years old when the Charlie came out. Back then, robots were the wave of the future, but they had yet to break shore. My parents would tell me later the Revolution came as a surprise. People expected robotics to gain ground, but slowly, inch by inch. That had been the story for the past century, why would now be any different? Obviously that was not the case.

Before Charlie, I had seen plenty of 'robots', but not what we would call robots today. There were robots that built cars, robots that performed surgeries… none of these had any autonomy or learning capability (at least not much). Frankly, even Charlie was primitive, but I say that in hindsight. The point I'm trying to get to is I had never seen a humanoid robot, at least not in person. By the time I was in high school, they were everywhere.

It's hard to describe how much changed in those years, though my own perspective was biased. Growing up, the emergence of robots was just part of my childhood. Yes, their rise was incredibly quick, but looking back, it seems almost normal. Still, even as a child, one facet of the situation alerted me to its abnormality: the unemployment crisis.

As most people know, the crisis cast a shadow over the entire Robotic Revolution. When you start to think about the numbers and the scale… it's absolutely mind-boggling. The Revolution caused a massive amount of fear and confusion. We've all heard about the riots, but the true depth of these things has been forgotten, overlooked in the wake of the Initiative and the countless positive outcomes that were yet to come. Put simply, everyone knows how many millions of jobs were lost, but we are more cognizant of the eventual solutions. The problem is, we forget just how long it took for these solutions to arrive.

Therein lies the first paradox of the robotic age. We yearned for robots to lower our own workload, but the workload was our paycheck. Meanwhile, the robot evangelists spoke of perfect healthcare and impartial police, but these jobs were far too complex to handle at the time. The only thing to be fully automatic and robotized was basic labor.

As an adolescent, I tried to avoid the ugly side of things, but that was impossible. I saw fights, arrests, the occasional mob—these are memories all of my generation shares. And of course the attacks on the robots themselves. It was a mess.

There was a turning point, somewhere in my early days of high school, where public opinion hit a record low. The Skellar case was in the news, and I remember seeing the Salt Lake City Riots on television, the burning of the McRay factory. Times were tense, but the only thing holding our economy together was the robotics industry itself. Or, at least, that's the impression I got at the time—I would probably trust the word of an economist over mine![3]

My own experience was privileged. My family was relatively well-off, particularly in regards to the Robotic Revolution. Both of my parents were lawyers, so the unemployment crisis didn't affect us directly. If anything, lawyers were in greater demand, and my parents had plenty of work. But my high school education was immediately shaped by these ongoing events. I graduated in 2105 and, like the rest of my generation, aimed for a university degree in robotics.

---

[3] According to Ellen Taylor (chapter 2), Dr. Thompson is mostly correct. More information can be found in her chapter.

The educational reforms were just getting started so they didn't really affect my experience, but I did apply overseas.[4] Oxford offered a general robotics degree, and I focused on cerebral units, though they were not known as such at the time. I won't go into too much detail about all of that, as many other works have done my academic career justice,[5] but I'd like to share a few thoughts about some of my classes.

For all of the non-core openings I had, I took robotics electives dealing with the political, social, and philosophical implications of the Revolution and the future of robotics. It was here that my idea of the Angel Paradigm began to form, although I cannot remember if it had yet been referred to as such. There were many issues that were covered in those days: cyborgs, androids, the definition of intelligence, the definition of consciousness, artificial love, etc. etc. But there are two in particular I want to mention as they have direct bearing on the Paradigm: human superiority and superintelligence.

With the advent of humanoid robots and the subsequent effects on the labor force, many people were wary of further robotic advancements. To make things worse, robots were increasing in intelligence at an amazing rate. This was great news for roboticists, but it tended to scare a lot of people, and not just because their job might be next. I remember when robots started to complement autopilots on aircraft, some carriers had to reverse the trend because people were afraid to fly under the complete control of computers. Now the whole system is built into the craft itself and no one bats an eye.

Superintelligence is still a hot issue today. The typically cited scenario goes as follows: humans develop an artificial general intelligence at or

---

[4] At the time, universities in the United States were typically expensive and operated more like a for-profit business than the education-focused institutions of present-day. This exacerbated the already-rampant unemployment issue, and would eventually lead to major educational reform. Educational reform is covered in more detail by Dr. Kyle Fix (chapter 7).

[5] See *The Evolution of Cerebral Units* by Randall Ticorra.

above human intelligence. This AI is capable of recursive self-improvement, leading to an exponential intelligence explosion known as the technological singularity. But there is a major weakness in this proposition: we still don't truly understand intelligence.

By some accounts, superintelligence is all around us. Most contemporary robots are vastly superior to humans at a multitude of tasks. The expected rate of recursive self-improvement is not quite there yet, but robots have already helped solve many of the most complicated problems in math and physics. So has the technological singularity passed, or is it still on the horizon?

Of course this question has no outright answer—only time will tell. Humans have thus far underestimated their importance in this phenomenon, as we have always been the authors of the code—even when the code gives our creation permission to become its own author. When the robot army comes knocking at your door, then you will truly know. Or perhaps there is a more nuanced, insidious plan? Or why must it be insidious? As you can see, these questions border on science fiction, and frankly, I see no reason to address them.

Continuing our discussion of human superiority (or lack thereof), it is interesting to note how our pride has come into play. For some reason, computers being good at math never seemed to bother too many people pre-millenium. Even self-driven cars didn't really cause any envy. But as soon as you put a computer in a humanoid body and it starts to do your job, it's not the same as a box of wires, even though objectively we should know it is.

All of these factors are integral to the Paradigm. How far do we let robots serve us if they begin to infringe on our self-worth? I will admit I am stretching a bit here, but only because I am saving the best for last. Remember that I mentioned there are two parts to the Paradigm: servitude and supervision. During these discussions on human superiority, the idea of supervision began to appear.

Put simply, at some point, robots will no longer serve us, but guide us. Let's go back to the idea of the aircraft—is the craft serving us or supervising us? The line is more blurred than you'd think, and it keeps going in that direction. Yes, we control the aircraft, its destination, speed, and the like, but in the end it controls our lives. Why else were all those early adopters forced to backtrack their plans?

Perhaps the most famous and interesting example that we discussed at Oxford was the robot judiciary. Could robots be programmed to pass judgement? Obviously this is a debate that continues to this day, and the independent morality problem is a huge stepping stone in making the scenario a possibility, so you can see how it caught my attention.

The potential benefit was always stated as 'the removal of the negative aspects of the human element in judgement.' First and foremost this meant corruption: the judiciary in the early millennium was steeped in human weaknesses. Laws were passed by lobbying interest groups, and the quality of a lawyer was based on their price; in other words, money could literally buy both regulations and verdicts, or at least heavily sway them in a certain direction.[6]

But what else would be taken away with robots? Maybe there would be less ambiguity in decision-making and a more clear adherence to the law? Unfortunately, thinking of these as benefits is ignoring what would most likely happen. Robots may not understand the complex circumstances of particular cases, leading to by-the-book rulings. So that's it, case closed, robots can't be lawyers and they definitely can't be judges, right?

Well, back then, you'd be right. But today? Robots aren't lawyers yet, and maybe they never will be, but they are finding their way into the system. Most law clerks are assisted by robots or are robots themselves, and of course robot involvement in the rehabilitation of offenders has changed the nature and variety of sentences. Right now the wall

---

[6] Different countries had somewhat different legislative and judiciary systems. Dr. Thompson is referring to the United States in particular, though these problems existed in many places.

preventing a robot from making judgements on its own is the independent morality problem. And if that wall comes down, we will find that it was in fact a dam, with an enormous amount of water behind it.

The first thing that happens is we run into the anthropomorphic paradox. As we begin to develop independent morality in robots, we do so with the purported purpose of bringing a more 'fair' or 'equal' morality into the decision-making process. The common idea is that human morality is, depending on the individual, lightly to heavily corrupted. But how do you think we are modeling the robot's morality? In many ways, we are trying to mimic human morality. Therein lies the paradox—we want a robot morality that isn't human (because of potential negative traits) but at the same time is human (because that is the basis of our understanding of morality itself). Right now robots aren't human enough to be in the judiciary, but can we reach a point where they become too human, and it doesn't make a difference?

In the end, all of this robotic involvement in decision-making is a type of supervision. The question is whether a hard line exists that won't be crossed. Is a robot judiciary going to make as much sense as auto-piloted aircraft do now, or is that a change we will resist forever? This is a central question to the Angel Paradigm, and Michael Trualt tried to take us over that line about ten years ago.

I joined UR in 2115, a few years after they had essentially ousted McRay. This was also around the time when Trualt was entering the public eye and the Initiative began to take form. I had the somewhat unique opportunity to meet and speak with Trualt a few times at UR. When I first joined, Trualt was the senior roboticist overseeing central processing, making him my boss's boss. At the time he was a well-respected executive and scientist, and a large part of UR's emerging success. No one really knew about his socio-political views, and I would argue that had they been known, he would not have been promoted to such a high level in the first place.

Over the course of my first three years, central processing managed to deliver the first functional prototype cerebral unit. Two years later, in 2120, we produced the first self-contained cerebral unit on the market, the Aurora. The media has always over-played my involvement in that process. It was a team of almost two hundred roboticists that worked tirelessly and succeeded together. I made some minor contributions, but I maintain that UR would have had its first cerebral unit by 2120 whether I had joined or not.

Meanwhile, Trualt exerted some level of influence in the marketing department, and our launch campaign managed to have an informal but clever political slant: United Robotics: The Future Is United.[7] Most of our commercials revolved around human cooperation via robotic assistance, which is in some ways the Angel Paradigm itself. The entire campaign was well-received, and I would call it the launch pad for what was to come.

In our larger meetings, Trualt was reserved, concise. This was my impression of him from the outset, and most of our early interactions cemented this reputation. I thought he shared the same stance as the rest of us: that robots would help unite the people of the world symbolically, not literally. Clearly, this did not turn out to be the case. I remember one time he had come to my lab to talk about some development or problem with Aurora—I can't recall what exactly—and he started telling me how we were about to change the world. What I took to be exaggerated enthusiasm turned out to be hints of the future.

It's hard to believe that between the release of the Aurora and the founding of the Earth Legislature only eight years passed. In those eight years, and really in the past eleven years, the world has changed more than it had in the previous century. The Initiative and Trualt's actions are the most relevant series of events related to the Paradigm, so I will give my own brief overview of it all. I would prefer to give a fully chronological

[7] This advertising campaign actually began in 2118, two years before the Aurora, but became famous with its relation to the Aurora.

account of everything that happened, but between all of the overlapping events and my own messy recollection, I will occasionally weave in a more topical approach. Even so, I may unintentionally omit quite a bit!

Obviously, as a relatively senior employee of UR, the Initiative took on a wholly different form than is usually described. However, like most of the public, I wasn't truly aware of the scope of what was happening until the dominos had already begun to fall. This hints at the genius of Trualt's actions, as nearly everything went according to his synchronized plan. Even though we never reached his ultimate goal of a robot-run society, we came much closer than I think anyone would have guessed back in 2120.

One of Trualt's most useful tools was the United Robotics Public Works Division. Created in 2106, it tackled many United States infrastructure projects and was a major reason for UR's early growth. Municipalities, counties, states, and eventually the federal government hired UR and its robots for millions of jobs at rates that quickly dropped below the human competition. By cementing these relationships early, UR was able to control a significant majority of all government-contracted robotic work. Trualt saw Public Works as his bridge to social engineering, and made himself well-known in the department. While his influence was felt in many of their projects, one was fundamentally tied to his plans.

Project Node began as an internal connectivity upgrade aimed at bringing massive speed boosts within and between our regional offices. With a little public relations push, the project crossed into Public Works and began upgrading the networks immediately around each office, then the encompassing city, and soon the nationwide snowball was a worldwide avalanche and we had telecommunications companies and foreign governments fighting us from all sides. Of course, this became a non-issue when the override occurred, but there was a time when UR was subject to an unprecedented barrage of lawsuits and court cases.

There were two major developments that came out of Project Node, the first of which was the creation of a foundation that would evolve into the Cloud.[8] The second development, based off of the first, was the creation of an effective communication network for all of UR's products across the globe. The only real evidence ever presented that tied Trualt to the inner workings of Project Node was the presence of extremely well-hidden accessibility software—software that interacted directly with the Athena—but we will delve into those details soon.

The Athena was the catalyst in Trualt's plans, the key to his worldwide coup. The military successor to the Aurora, the Athena was a much more advanced cerebral unit with an almost undetectable flaw: a commanding override function accessible only by Trualt himself. Now a typical cerebral unit has no traditional wireless capability—wireless robot communications are encrypted and sent over a proprietary protocol. For the Athena, this wireless capability was tweaked slightly to allow secure military control, but the premise was the same. Normally, once a company produces a robot and starts its lifecycle, that company only has access to a fail-safe remote shutdown, a call-back function, co-owner or co-government authorized live positioning, and certain diagnostics. For the Athena, most of these functions were removed or placed under military control, but Trualt managed to hide his administrative override in the now supposedly empty channel.

In the course of working on over a dozen models of cerebral units, I would never doubt the ability of our team to catch such a glaring inconsistency. However, it was the military's own desire for information compartmentalization that allowed Trualt to plant his program. As the senior roboticist of central processing, Trualt was the only one granted access to the entirety of the Athena. Sure, there were a few military roboticists thrown in for security purposes, but cerebral unit technology was brand new, a creation of our team that no other roboticist in the

[8] It is perhaps easier to understand the barrage of litigation if one considers that a private corporation, United Robotics, was keen on controlling the worldwide communication network. Even if it was not the Cloud as it exists today, this would still pose a serious threat to net neutrality and of course national sovereignty.

world had managed to duplicate. For all intents and purposes, it was beyond their comprehension.

From my standpoint, it was a terribly frustrating build. We were able to use many parts of the Aurora as a foundation, but the number and complexity of the desired or required changes made the military's strict construction guidelines a colossal waste of time. Most of the time we were implementing changes we thought were unnecessary, hoping they were related to a change being made somewhere else in the chain. The irony in all of this was the military's line of reasoning: by spreading the workload in a convoluted manner, no one roboticist would have compromising knowledge of the overall Athena code. The universe has an odd sense of humor.

Despite relying heavily on the already-functioning Aurora, the Athena took nearly three years to develop. We began major shipments in 2122, starting with a six-thousand unit order by the United States Army. Demand was unprecedented. At the time of the override in 2124, the Athena controlled a force of three million robots spread across the globe.

Over the preceding decade, the Angel Paradigm had emerged as a cultural phenomenon. Scholars and laymen debated the implications of a robot-guided future, and where the line should, would, or could be drawn. One major argument rose against the use of the Athena and military robotics in general, as this favored dependent development rather than independent development—in other words, military robots were being programmed to be more and more controlled by humans rather than self-controlled. The Angel Paradigm typically sided with an independent view, as dependent robots would of course be more biased by their owners or masters. Ironically, Trualt argued this point as well, but ended up being the master of millions of robots at once!

The strongest idea that emerged from discussions involving the Paradigm was the Earth Initiative. Influential scientists and several politicians mulled over the conceptual possibility of a united Earth, putting forth a framework proposal for an Earth Legislature, Earth

Presidents, and Earth Court. These Initiators—as they would come to be known—often put themselves in a compromising position: politicians had to toe the line of patriotism, while scientists in specific fields could be moved, demoted, or even fired for their view.

Trualt was smart enough to never reveal himself as an Initiator, but his position on the matter became more and more clear in the years approaching the override. He would argue for the spread of robots in previously-prohibited ventures, and promoted a borderline radical globalist approach to our work, claiming at one point the cerebral unit should be made open source. Just as we, the employees, started to see what he was thinking, the first assassination attempt took place.

I'd rather not get into the details of that particular event, but I will say for a few weeks our entire department at UR was in a state of shock. We assumed Trualt had been targeted due to his involvement with the Athena, either by some aggressive nation-state or an anti-military psychopath. Truthfully, the Athena was the most likely motivation and the nation-state conjecture remains up for debate, but the details remain a mystery to this day. In any case, he had anticipated this move, and his robots were not only able to protect him, but to record the event itself. And that was the catalyst for the Initiative.

There are conflicting definitions of the Earth Initiative. Officially, it coincides with January 1st, 2128, when the Earth Government took power. But Trualt's override command occurred in April of 2124, and the three plus years in between are arguably more important. In fact, I would say the Initiative isn't over yet. Initiative-resistance is alarmingly common, and the world is desperately trying to adjust to such drastic, rapid change. This resistance should come as no surprise. In fact, the level of adherence is far more surprising, although that can be partially attributed to the Initiators.

To this day I am asked or assumed to be one of them (particularly due to my current position as Chair of the Robotics Committee), but I assure you that is not the case. Of course, most of the remaining Initiators refuse to go public, and many are under constant threat, so I can't blame the public for their disbelief in my statement. However, the Initiators were almost exclusively chosen[9] for their strategic influence—their ability to uphold the Initiative as it unfolded. While I was heavily involved in UR and cerebral units, I had little political sway, and frankly, Trualt ran the show on our stage.

I did receive one of the infamous preemptive robot messages, and knew a few hours before he activated his embedded control program that something was about to happen. All of these memories are vivid. One of the robots in our department came up to me around nine in the morning and announced the coming crisis with stunning indifference, then proceeded in its daily tasks. After digesting the ramblings, I assumed it was some sort of bizarre prank and continued working, confused if not troubled. I didn't quite connect the dots between the robot's message and the assassination attempt two months earlier, but they were connected for me soon enough.

In the blink of an eye, three million of the most advanced robots ever created were placed in the hands of one man. It was not immediately clear what had happened. Within minutes of the override, we had thousands of calls from military installations and government officials asking us what was going on. Every branch of the military and seemingly half of its intelligence organizations—including the NSA, CIA, and FBI—were at our main offices within minutes. For the first hour, our entire company went into a panic. We tried to look back over the Athena code only to find the project totally wiped from existence, all files erased beyond recovery. We would later learn our own robots had been programmed to do this in the hours before the override. The FBI was questioning everyone, and all of our offices across the nation were put on lockdown.

---

[9] Although there is no conclusive evidence on the matter, a popular hypothesis is that Trualt organized most of the Initiators himself, letting them know of his plans ahead of time.

Meanwhile, the Initiators came out in full force, paving the way for a global movement that would become the Earth Initiative. If I tried to explain everything that happened in the following weeks, even just from my own perspective, I would probably double the length of your book. There are thousands upon thousands of books, papers, and articles regarding the three and a half years between the override and the founding of the Legislature—I will focus on the main events related to my own experience and the Angel Paradigm.

My fellow employees and I were finally released about sixteen hours after the override, under strict supervision. This was a short-sighted gesture, as the intelligence and criminal agencies were running thin, but at this point they were still not sure who to blame. With the volatile nature of events in those first few days, the supervision would wane and eventually disappear—they had much bigger problems than confused roboticists.

The Athena models did not stand about idly. Trualt, likely with the help of many hundreds of Initiators, had envisioned thousands of missions for these robots which they immediately and dutifully attended to. No corners were cut: I've heard many stories about groups of robots disappearing at just the right moment, or continuing to work as programmed for a few extra minutes just so they could sneak away undetected. Obviously, the factor of surprise lasted only a few moments, and there were several instances of minor skirmishes between humans and/or older models with the Athena models. But in most cases, the robots either used their superior strength or their superior intellect, gaining leverage however possible.

The intricacies of execution here are beyond Trualt or any of the Initiators, but that is not a surprise. Given the command to complete their new missions without allowing themselves to come to harm, the robots could use their terrific reasoning skills to determine the most efficient way to make it happen. What's surprising is how many robots were eventually stopped.[10]

Once the true scale of events became apparent, a certain level of chaos erupted. Governments went on the hunt for the robots and of course their creators, hence the national lockdown on UR. But thanks to the Initiators, it was mostly useless. Significant portions of the populations of wealthier nations were already calling for global unification. The Athena models vowed to enforce this as-of-yet non-existent power and, being military robots, they had the ability to subdue and even harm humans. Unfortunately, this ability was exercised early and often.

The main missions given to the robots were related to decreasing military effectiveness. They commandeered highly secure networks and rendered millions of weapons useless or inert. As the pinnacle of military prowess, the robots themselves faced little that they couldn't handle, but most governments and military entities refused to part with their power. This led to many small-scale struggles, and a few larger ones. Again, I'm afraid I must gloss over most of the details if we are to focus on the Angel Paradigm itself, but suffice to say that by the end of one year, it was all but decided.

Now I do want to emphasize (and this has been said before by many) that when I spoke of the chaos the override wrought, it faded extremely quickly. Sure, things didn't settle down for that first year—honestly, they still haven't—but the drop off was noticeable. The Initiators were spreading their plans with incredible speed, and they were not only coherent, but remarkably sane. Proof of the Athena and Trualt's motives was made clearer every day, and the initial rumors of a worldwide coup by a crazed roboticist were rather quickly relegated to the typical conspiracy enthusiasts.[11] Of course, in some ways, the sheer efficiency of it all,

---

[10] Estimates range from 2000 to 4000, depending on the applicable time frame.

[11] These theories may have originated from intelligence agencies themselves, and some still believe we are now under the control of a select elite.

between the robots and the Initiators, made it highly suspicious. But there was little anyone could do at that point but trust the people behind the wheel.

Meanwhile, Trualt's relationship with United Robotics had some interesting effects on our company and my own career. At the time of the override, I was a relatively senior-level cerebral unit programmer, and had a few teams under my supervision. However, I was not at all involved in the business side of things, and so I don't know too much about the level of cooperation between Trualt and UR's top executives before the override. Whether they had planned this together from the beginning, or they had simply gotten a prerecorded message like my own, I do not know. But once UR was taken off lockdown, about one month after the override, the company announced our official support for the Earth Initiative and Trualt. It helped that during the month lockdown, most of the board and highest executives had resigned and been replaced. In addition, Trualt himself formally resigned, and pledged that the Athena models were not an army under UR's control.

Once UR returned, we spun the story that even though we had broken our promise to their clients by allowing the Athena to come under the control of Trualt, in the end it was for the greater good of humanity. Normally this would be preposterous, but again, the public was riding the wave of the Paradigm. Frankly, just talking about this makes me realize how surprising those years were.

As for me personally, I had mixed feelings about it all, but it was hard to ignore the information given to us by Trualt and the Initiators. They had realistic plans and were pursuing them aggressively. I waited for the day Trualt would turn the Athena against us and try to take over the world, but I knew soon enough this would never happen. I let myself be cautiously optimistic, and in the end it paid off.

When UR came back online, I was asked to replace our vice president of central processing, who had moved up to take Trualt's position. Our Athena successor was scrapped, and we were focused on the successor to the Aurora. In more ways than I thought possible, life went on as usual. We revived our five year old marketing campaign, The Future Is United, proudly embracing the Earth Initiative. In many ways, it was an exciting time. But our company was seen in one of two ways: as the builders of the robots that would propel humanity to a brighter future, or as the unstoppable elite force that used the robots and the Initiative as a road to ultimate power. And while I will say we were more of the former, that doesn't mean we weren't the latter. Several of the top executives were using the Initiative and our involvement to pursue record profits, but Trualt used this greed as a tool. As long as his vision of a more united future came to be, he didn't mind if people did it selflessly or selfishly.

About one year after the override, in the summer of 2125, the Earth Government began to take shape. Here, finally, we saw a true glimpse of the Angel Paradigm according to Trualt, as well as the fascinating inner struggle within the high ranks of the Initiators. Over the preceding decade, many of the Initiators and countless political scientists discussed, debated, and dissected possible worldwide government systems. A few options stood out as particularly plausible, and at the core of it all was the Earth Legislature.

There were differing opinions on how to distribute the representatives and whether to have unicameral, bicameral, etc. but most intriguing of all was the Robotic Assembly Proposal. Trualt himself was not interested in an Earth Legislature run by humans, he was ready to see the robots write our laws. The Robotic Assembly Proposal outlined an Earth Legislature composed of law-making robots with human support and correction. At its core was the idea of eventual human removal from the process as legislative robots evolved to prove themselves worthy. Clearly, Trualt believed in a radical but pure form of the Angel Paradigm, and was trying to use his position of power to see it become reality.

The Proposal met with enormous opposition from the more powerful Initiators. They had envisioned their own rise to power through the Initiative, and were planning to place themselves within the governmental framework. Trualt predicted this outcome, and was able to fight the Initiators at their own propaganda game, generating a wave of public condemnation of the Initiator's plans. What was perhaps most surprising was the level of support he gathered for the Proposal itself, although with robot acceptance at a peak, if it was ever going to happen, that was the time.

All of this disagreement began a protracted struggle, and was one of the main reasons the Earth Initiative did not take hold for nearly three more years. While Trualt had the Athena models and a large portion of the public on his side, he was not in a position of absolute power. For the duration of the Initiative, Trualt's most valuable asset was his honesty. From the beginning, everything he had done or planned was made known to the general public, and he preached a new culture of truth. Perhaps his most important pledge, and one that garnered the most approval, was his refusal to use the Athena models as his private army. He went out of his way to prove this was the case, and any sort of pressure on the Initiators from the robots would have been met with swift and devastating criticism from the people. In addition, many of these dissenting Initiators were essential to his original success, and despite their apparent corruption, Trualt was not going to ignore their previous contribution.

I am constantly in awe of how lucky we were. Most humans cannot be truly responsible with power. As much as I'd love to think I would follow Trualt's path, if I were given control of the Athena force, would I wield it as gently? But that was not the fault in his thinking. Yes, humans are frustratingly corrupt. But that does not mean robots are the answer. This was essentially the argument presented by the other Initiators, and it was the argument that slowly convinced the public. Over time, the Proposal evolved, and there were years of discussion on finding a balance between robot and human control. The Earth Legislature became less and less robotic, until it was finally decided to have fully human legislature, with practically no robotic involvement.[12]

To Trualt's credit, he followed public opinion. Although he spoke often of the error in our decision, he agreed to uphold it in full. The silver lining was that this further proved his honesty, and gave a significant boost to pro-Initiative sentiment. While the legislative debate was underway, other facets of the Earth Government were discussed and finalized so that by the end of 2127, the Earth Initiative was ready to take effect.

With the demise of the Robotic Assembly Proposal, a key facet of the Angel Paradigm was left out of the Earth Initiative, but there were many other areas where robotic involvement was heavily increased. Here I will definitely have to leave out the details, as a lot of the changes that were made were economic in nature (again, I direct you to an economist!) but I can certainly comment on their relation to the Paradigm and my company.

For starters, industries that were already heavily robotized had two new avenues of expansion: the first was true globalization, covering or attempting to cover those regions that were unable or unwilling to afford robotization before, and the second was an additional layer of robotization, e.g. programming robot supervisors for robot manufacturers. In addition, a few of the more difficult industries that had yet to be robotized, would now be brought under the umbrella by the advances in technology. All of this meant the Angel Paradigm was expanding in both vectors concurrently—service and supervision. Public opinion was so positive, however, that there was little to no opposition to the forward march of robotics.

To supply this newfound demand, UR worked on Aurora II, which would eventually become Eirene, our current top model. With our admittedly monopolistic position, we were able to standardize the cerebral unit in the years between the override and the Initiative. That being said,

---

12 At the legislative level. There was (and is) a great deal of robotic involvement at the lower-administrative level.

there was more than enough demand to go around, and after Trualt put pressure on our top-level executives, we made most of our findings and research open-source.

Then all of the sudden it was December 31st, 2127, and a worldwide celebration began to commemorate the beginning of the Initiative. If I could relive that day, I would. I know there were protests and disagreements, but for the most part, it really did seem like the world was united, and robotics was the cause. Despite all of the flaws, despite the morally ambiguous path we took, I was and am proud to be a part of the industry that drove us toward a more humane (and robotic) future. Yes, I wish some things had been handled differently, but the results speak for themselves.

At midnight GMT, the start of 2128, the Earth Initiative officially took effect. Over the previous year, Michael Trualt had sent over a million Athena models back to UR for disassembly and recycling. On the eve of our united Earth, as a symbolic gesture of the progress we had made and to show the world he could give them the same level of trust he was given, he brought his personal escort force to UR and left them for disassembly. It was the first time we had seen him in person in over three years, and he had gone from an eccentric boss to a global phenomenon. The whole thing was surreal.

I managed to speak to him for a few moments before he held his major press conference, and though they were simply pleasantries, I will never forget that conversation. He had changed, as a person. There was hope within him, but it was buried by responsibility. Something about giving up his escort seemed to give him a measure of relief, and I will forever be grateful to have seen the hint of happiness in his expression in those final moments.

It's difficult for me to speak about the press conference. I was not there, but I was in the building so I witnessed the aftermath. To this day, I am ashamed. Ashamed of my species for allowing us to get so far and then doing something like that. When the alarms went off I knew what had happened. I think everyone knew it was going to happen, but not so soon. Michael Trualt was without his personal escort for less than two hours before he was shot dead. The man who had championed the Angel Paradigm was gone, but he had done his share. Rest in peace.

There was a week of mourning and some compounded tragedies as several terroristic groups attempted to use his assassination as a springboard for anarchy. Thankfully, the remaining Athena models managed to suppress the rebellion, and the Initiators and Earth Government proved themselves able to handle the situation.

With growing concern that cerebral scanning was not sufficient in stopping robotic crime, the Bureau of Robotic Affairs was founded in 2129. At almost the exact same time, the ever-evolving Earth Legislature passed a resolution to create a new Robotics Committee, and voted me in as Chair. This came as a surprise, but I accepted the offer, as it allowed me to have more impact with my experience and did not prevent my research from continuing. I had to relinquish my vice president position and become an affiliated researcher, but this meant I replaced my executive duties at UR with legislative duties of the Earth, and that just sounds better, doesn't it?

In the four years since, I've been able to focus more and more on the independent morality problem and hopefully make some reasonable decisions involving the state of robotics on Earth, but of course I'm biased for myself so who knows.

As for how I feel about the Angel Paradigm, I think I can summarize for you quite nicely. The Paradigm brought us through the Initiative, which was the single-most beneficial development in humankind in the past century, maybe more. In that sense, it has been a blessing. And as I have said before, we were incredibly lucky to have Michael Trualt leading the way, but he too made mistakes, and we must be careful not to fall into the same traps. Robots will help us, and robots will guide us, but the future must be mankind's, let's not forget that.

2. Ellen Taylor, Economist - - Written Correspondence[1]

Dr. Taylor specializes in Labor Economics with a focus on Robots and Automation. As an economic advisor of the Earth Initiative, she helped shape the current global economic landscape. She now acts as a Senior Advisor to the Economics Committee of the Earth Legislature.

Robotic development, from the turn of the millennium through present day, has been entrenched in international economics. What began as the simple automation of labor became an unprecedented economic crisis. This crisis never truly subsided, and stability was only found after an overhaul of global policies landed us with the Earth Initiative. So much is common knowledge.

The Angel Paradigm was the philosophical mantra of Michael Trualt, a complicated idea behind a simple facade: humans alone are incapable of a fair and peaceful society, but robots can get us there. The Paradigm was the foundation of the Initiative, but realism defeated idealism, bringing us closer to Trualt's vision without breaking down society. This is also well known.

But these summaries do little to portray the sheer scale of economic change that has occurred in the past thirty years and do nothing at all to hint at the potential of the future. What follows is a more in-depth look at the economic implications of the Angel Paradigm from the turn of the millennium to the near and distant future.

Before continuing, it is worth noting the massive differences between the field of robotics circa 2000 and the field of robotics today. Most of the disparity comes from the definition of what a robot is: in 2000, a robot was a mechanical agent, typically an electromagnetic machine, that was guided by programming and/or circuitry. Today, there are two types of robots: semi to fully autonomous humanoid machines and semi to fully

[1] Received 09.12.2133. Current form approved by Dr. Taylor 12.03.2134.

autonomous computers. Ever since the Revolution, the line of autonomy that separates robots from other machines has steadily risen, and continues to rise. In summary, a robot in 2000 would be considered a machine today, as will be readily apparent based on following descriptions.

With this in mind, around the year 2000, the field of robotics was growing rapidly but sporadically. There were many different types of robots doing many different tasks in many different ways—it would be impossible to list them all here. In the first half of the 21st century, progress was promising but always just below expectations. Early roboticists and enthusiasts predicted certain levels of autonomy or intelligence by a certain date, but they were often disappointed. This, at least, has not changed.

The Angel Paradigm itself follows the same pattern of unfulfilled expectations. The idyllic vision of a peaceful, carefree, robot-driven existence that emerged well before the Revolution would eventually become the complex Paradigm of present day. Most of these dreams were devoid of any economic variables whatsoever, where robots took care of things and somehow money simply vanished from the equation. Reality is not as simple. In fact, it is at times unforgivingly complex, and this truth came to light as the Paradigm evolved.

By the 2050s, the main markets affected by robotics were manufacturing, transportation, and agriculture. However, none of these markets used humanoid robots. Manufacturing had perfected robotic arms, most of the transportation infrastructure was now based on self-driving cars, and in agriculture, specially-designed robots performed everything from harvesting to weed removal. There were certainly great strides made in other areas—notably robotic surgery—but the impact and spread of robots was most pronounced in those three fields.

The only exception to this generalization would be the military. It was military interests that provided the greatest deal of funding and research to robotics, particularly in the United States. Drones were the most mature field, with robot soldiers also in the works. This line of research would become an important reason for United Robotics's close relationship with the military, but not for another half-century.

In 2077, Seth McRay founded his now-famous company as a robotic arm venture trying to expand the hardware and software of manufacturing arms into other fields, particularly the medical field. What started as a crossover between manufacturing and medicine grew into an outright mess of niche markets. Propelled by early success with the medical arms, McRay managed to purchase almost one hundred other robotics companies operating in at least thirty markets. Sometime around 2090, the idea for the mass-produced humanoid base model came about, and in 2096 McRay released the Charlie and the Robotic Revolution began.

Meanwhile, the crisis of technological unemployment had already begun to take hold. Many argued that automation would raise productivity and increase income, generating demand for more products and services, and thus create jobs to replace the ones taken by automation. But even in 2050, this was not the case. Wages versus the cost of living had been stagnant or even dropping for decades. Labor was being replaced by capital, and owners of capital took on a larger and larger portion of the world's wealth. The gap between the rich and the poor widened every day, and there were many small-scale attempts to fix the problem but it took the Revolution to spark the social fire.

In the first year after the Charlie came out, twenty million jobs were lost in the United States and 300 million were lost worldwide. McRay saw phenomenal profits and was making new specialization builds every week. Cashiers, clerks, a significant portion of the food service industry, as well as material movers, such as truck loaders and baggage handlers, and janitors and other cleaners were almost completely replaced. This started with the larger corporations that could afford the robots and quickly transitioned to middle-sized businesses. Only the smallest companies kept these sorts of employees.

While many jobs opened up in the robotics industry, that was far from a solution to the problem. A few wealthy owners ran each business, and they had millions of people desperate for a salary, even if it was kept low. The number of new jobs was four orders of magnitude lower than the number of jobs lost: approximately ten thousand openings for each one hundred million closings.

With the severe cut in employment came a new wave of Luddism, and most of the social unrest in the first few years was aimed squarely at the robotics industry itself. The Paradigm, though it didn't exist by the name just yet, seemed to be a lie—robots had arrived, but life wasn't easier. In fact, many had questioned the idyllic visions from the start. Over a hundred years before the Robotic Revolution, the well-known economist John Maynard Keynes predicted 15-hour workweeks in 2030. But 2030 came and went, and workweeks had barely changed. Now it was seventy years beyond 2030, the workweek was almost the same, and wages were dropping.

As it turns out, there was a force constricting the Paradigm, preventing it from emerging in a realistic fashion. This force was a combination of socio-cultural norms, specifically the beliefs surrounding production, consumption, and a living wage. The aforementioned gap between capital and labor, the rich and the poor, was being fed by an over-producing and over-consuming society. In the 21st century, individuals were expected to work to make a living, and many Paradigm-related policies were labelled socialist (at the time, this was occasionally a negative term). But the Revolution saw the tide finally shifting.

In the United States, the economic situation was initially addressed by the Basic Income Expansion of 2101. Basic income or guaranteed income started when the government, against heavy opposition, passed the original Basic Income Act of 2043. In simple terms, a basic income is a societal allowance which is usually viewed as either a redistribution of wealth or country-wide joint ownership but is really both. The basic income established by the United States in 2043 found most of its funding by merging almost every other financial aid program currently in existence, from Social Security (by then already outdated) to Medicaid and most forms of federal welfare. The original intent was to trim down the bureaucracy and streamline the system, with the added possibility of cutting out a certain amount of poverty. Every month, each citizen of the United States would receive about $1000—the exact amount changed yearly with inflation—to use as they please.

While it was far from perfect, and the bureaucracy was certainly not eradicated, the Basic Income Act was a surprising success. Most notably, within the first decade of basic income, the number of families and individuals below the official poverty line declined by 74%.

The greatest concern regarding the Act was whether it would incentivize not working, and in some regards, it did. However, over 90% of those who chose not to work did not sit idly: for example, the Basic Income Act provided for realistic maternity and paternity leave, as well as caregiving capabilities for sick or disabled relatives or friends.

Through 2096, the Basic Income Act was more than enough to handle the level of technological unemployment in the United States economy. However, with the advent of the Robotic Revolution and the loss of twenty million jobs within a year's time, there was an urgent need for an increase in the basic income. The only problem was determining how to fund this rather large expansion.

The Basic Income Expansion of 2101 addressed this issue by essentially imposing taxes on the robotics industry. Major loopholes—including outsourcing manufacturing—were preemptively closed, and a corporation's punishment for evading their 'duty to society' was significantly heavier than simple compliance. The monthly payment more than doubled, passing the average living wage of the United States. In theory, a citizen of the United States could now survive without a job and be sustained by other factors, specifically the profits of the robotics industry. This of course began a number of legal disputes between robotics corporations and the government, particularly McRay. In the coming decade, this would contribute to their eventual downfall: when the government emerged as one of the major consumers of robotic labor, they bypassed McRay and chose up-and-coming United Robotics as their primary supplier.

With basic income now matching the living wage, Keynes's prediction edged a bit closer to reality. The gap between the holders of capital and laborers was narrowed by this legislation, allowing for a shorter work week and, in most cases, job flexibility. Depending on one's desired total income, there was a choice to do something for money or simply follow a passion. This was a milestone in the Angel Paradigm, as it suggests a society where one is free to work as one pleases.

However, it was not an all-encompassing solution. For all of the loopholes avoided, new ones would pop up, and most robotics companies made a point to pursue them aggressively. More importantly, the basic income was almost exclusively a United States program, but the whole world was feeling the effects of technological unemployment. While several other countries would implement similar programs, the unemployment crisis would continue for many years, and its effects are arguably still being felt today.

One of the more interesting but unsurprising developments concurrent with this legislation was the increase in price for non-robotic goods. The then-emerging market of human goods and services demanded an often significantly higher price than their robotic counterpart. This would augment the already-existing gap between hand-made and manufactured goods, but also included services, such as restaurants waited by human versus robot staff.

The next major economical reform in the United States was the Fair Care Act of 2112, which dramatically reduced the price of healthcare and, for most people, eliminated the need for insurance. While the final bill was significantly different from the original (the name was changed from Free Care to Fair Care), it was still seen as the second major step in the utopian direction.[2] The bill also marked the beginning of robotic acceptance, with public opinion starting to support their use and ubiquity, mostly due to the new association of robotics with free of near-free healthcare.

While the political implications of the Fair Care Act are noteworthy, the economic implications are equally important. In drastically simplified terms, healthcare transactions in the United States prior to the Fair Care Act involved providers, customers, and insurers. In theory, a customer would pay an insurance rate in exchange for reasonable prices when paying a provider. In practice, a convoluted relationship between the insurers and providers made prices anything but reasonable. There were quite a few other factors at play, including the involvement of the government as one insurance option, but this still presents a basic idea of the situation.

The Fair Care Act took advantage of the revolutionary circumstances of the newly robotized economy. On the production side, healthcare manufacturing was almost entirely robotic. Beyond the product materials themselves, manufacturers had to pay for the upfront cost of the robots, along with their maintenance. At first this made little difference, as robots and their maintenance matched the expense of human labor, but within the first decade, manufacturing prices were dropping and profits were soaring.

On the service side, much of the daily administration and labor of hospitals and clinics was made robotic, and even a portion of nurse and doctor responsibilities were taken up by robots. This portion of responsibilities was a far cry from the medical robots of present day, but it was revolutionary at the time. Here, the initial cost was also prohibitive, but as with manufacturing, prices decreased over time. The drop was not as drastic, but it was significant, especially coupled with the continued advancement and therefore continued addition of responsibilities. In other

---

[2] The evolution of robotic healthcare is covered in more detail by Dr. Casey Mooden (chapter 5).

words, while medical robots decreased in price, they increased in ability and versatility, only adding to their value.

With production and service profit soaring but almost no change in consumer pricing, the public began to scrutinize the healthcare industry. Exponential automation coupled with widening profit margins was a trend across many industries, but the public was most aware of it with respect to healthcare. After all, healthcare was one of the major selling points of the robotics industry, and once inquiring minds noted that it could be made extremely cheap, the political response was unprecedented. Production-wise, the Fair Care Act put a cap on markups, creating an immediate drop in the prices of healthcare products. An enormous number of procedures were quickly made affordable, and only a few specific situations that warranted a greater deal of human involvement required insurance.

The Fair Care Act was hailed by many as the beginning of an age of luxury, but most of the healthcare industry, as well as the dying health insurance industry, spent the next fifteen years—all the way up to the Initiative—fighting it with more urgency than the robotics corporations had fought the Basic Income Expansion. Many doctors and other medical professionals left the United States for more lucrative positions elsewhere, but their options were limited. The wealthier nations were all leaning on more socialist, robotic systems. Eventually some of these individuals opened private clinics catering to anti-robot and/or wealthy clients.

In terms of the Angel Paradigm, the Fair Care Act brought robotics to the forefront of human healthcare, something that brought the concept to life. It was in the years after the Fair Care Act that the Angel Paradigm really grew into a widely-known and discussed idea. While the Basic Income Act and Expansion were related to the shifting economic landscape, their connection to robotics was hidden beneath government workings. With the Fair Care Act, people were seeing robots whenever they went to the doctor.

From an economic standpoint, the emerging Angel Paradigm reshaped the way we think about the production of wealth, and even brought the post-scarcity economy into serious discussion. Based on how society has progressed into the present day, it is clear that these discussions were in some ways premature and in others prescient.

Top economists began to consider the possibility of a global political landscape, and how that would affect the economy. In simplified and unsurprising terms, the consensus reached by all of this investigation was that the global economy would have to arise slowly, as a gradual transition from the international economy. However, some variables were simply beyond control.

In 2124, Michael Trualt sent the override command to the three million active Athena robots. The next four years were a political and economic minefield, culminating in the official start of the Earth Initiative on January 1st of 2128. It would be impossible to list all of the changes that occurred in those four years, but there are several of note.

First, it is important to understand that the military power of three million robots was not what brought about the Initiative. While the Athena models were critical, it was the Initiators that actually performed the transition.

Spread throughout the power structure of the developed world, the Initiators were the champions of Trualt's vision. Many questions still remain, however, as to their nature and number. The moniker came during the Initiative, and it has been applied to anyone in a position of influence that directly or indirectly aided in global unification. Many of the Initiators were clearly working together, and many were clearly working with Trualt, but some were simply given that name by association.

For example, in the decade leading up to the override, several individuals and groups researched the economics that would support the emerging Earth Initiative. Almost all of them were eventually labeled Initiators.[3] The reason for this was simple: research ventures related to the

---

[3] Dr. Taylor finished her doctorate and joined the National Bureau of Economic Research in 2114. NBER officially aligned with the Initiators in 2126, although they had been unofficially affiliated for at least a decade prior.

Initiative began at a small and hypothetical scale but soon overtook all other major projects in nearly every economic institute across the globe. But just how that came about—and who was responsible—are questions that remain unanswered.

Because the override brought about an immediate and massive power shift, there was a shock through global markets. The Initiators anticipated this, to an extent, and lobbied for the immediate, official support of the United Nations. The UN's relationship with the World Bank Group, World Trade Organization, and International Monetary Fund made it a critical ingredient in the transition to a global economy.

However, not only was the entire situation still viewed by many people as a terroristic act, but the Initiators stipulated that the security council be dissolved and the UN agree to monumental structural changes over an incredibly short timeline. This threatened to halt the process, leaving markets in turmoil. But the WBG, WTO, and IMF were full of Initiators, as was the UN. By some estimates, Initiators made up half of the General Assembly. Altogether, this meant the delay was just that—a delay. Less than a year after the override, on March 1st of 2125, the United Nations officially aligned with the Initiative.

In the United States, drastic demilitarization coupled with heavy Initiator influence in Congress brought a diversion of funds toward education, infrastructure, and health and human services, among other departments. Most notably, the Basic Income was immediately doubled while taxes were lowered. Approval ratings reached record highs, despite a vocal dissenting minority.

Similar economic policies across the globe, particularly with regards to demilitarization, allowed the UN to emerge as the major avenue of Initiative political power. As the effects of these new policies began to reach the general population, it was hailed by some as the beginning of the Angel Paradigm. Public opinion of the Earth Initiative continued to improve, and Trualt and the Initiators became heroes of sorts.

With these changes, the sociopolitical climate began to stabilize and, by extension, the global economy. The credit was introduced as a global currency in June of 2126 and officially replaced all sovereign currencies at the start of the Initiative.

Of course, not everything went as smoothly as planned. Disagreements began to emerge between Trualt and the majority of the Initiators with regards to the future global economic structure. Trualt wanted to implement a participatory economic system with decentralized economic planning and common ownership of the means of production. On the surface this went hand in hand with his ideals of equity and solidarity, but they remained just that: ideals. This is not to say his suggestions were shallow: Trualt had a good grasp of what would be required in order to bring about this economy and a relatively cohesive plan to achieve it.

The problem lay in the balance of power. As mentioned earlier, the Earth Initiative did not come about due to the Athena force, it came about thanks to the Initiators. These radical economic policies posed a threat to the Initiators and their socioeconomic advantage. If Trualt attempted to enact his vision without the support of the Initiators, the Earth Initiative would fall apart. In the end, he was forced to abandon most of his economic policies in order to see the Initiative through.

While this can be seen, in a certain sense, as a case of greed or corruption, it was also one of common sense. The economy was already under enormous stress from the override and its results. Attempting to institute a radical economic system with a new global government was simply too much.

But the economic system was not the only disagreement Trualt had with the Initiators. A similar issue came up with the new planetary legislature. Where most Initiators saw a transition from the UN to the Earth Legislature, Trualt wanted a fully robotic legislature. Here the Initiators were able to sway public opinion in their favor, and Trualt was forced to give up yet another of the more radical pieces of his vision.

In May of 2127, the Earth Initiative was announced to take place at the start of the new year. The United Nations would disband, with most of its members moving on to roles in the new Earth government. Basic income programs across the globe meshed together to create the Life Fund, paid for mostly by the robotics industry. This too had its concessions, as the Life Fund reached about 70% of what Trualt had envisioned.[4]

On January 1st, 2128, the Earth Initiative officially took hold. At this point, the credit was relatively stable, and most economic metrics indicated a surprisingly positive outlook.

Almost five years have passed since that day and, given the circumstances, the economy has fared remarkably well. The success of the Initiative looks to continue, but the future of the Angel Paradigm is questionable.

Public opinion of robots and robotics has been waning since 2126. The consensus is that the robots have brought about a turning point in human history, but they now threaten to overshadow its future. From a philosophical standpoint, increases in robot intelligence and ubiquity foreshadow strong AI or AI takeover. But from an economic standpoint, a post-scarcity society will not be possible if further automation is stifled.

Within the Economics Committee of the Earth Legislature, these debates are a daily occurrence. While the current trend still favors automation, the support is clearly decreasing with each legislative cycle. With these trends in mind, it can be surmised that the Angel Paradigm is falling out of favor. What that means for the economy, for the Initiative, and for humanity remains to be seen.

---

[4] At its inception, the Life Fund gave 1000 credits per month to all registered humans of Earth. This value has changed over time to reflect changes in the market.

3. Anthony Livingston, Social Psychologist - - Unedited Interview[1]

Dr. Livingston is Chair of the Department of Psychology at Yale University. Widely known for his research in human/robot relationships and psychology, he has published over seventy articles and written three books on the subject. He is currently writing a fourth book on artificial love.

AUTHOR: Good morning, Dr. Livingston.

DR. LIVINGSTON: Hello. Good morning!

AUTHOR: Thank you again for taking the time to speak with me. Your input is extremely valuable.

DR. LIVINGSTON: *(laughs)* Of course. This is one of my favorite subjects in robot, or, well, human and robot psychology. And I'm a huge — I really support the way you are putting this info together. Seems like a lot of work.

AUTHOR: I'm sure it will be worth it.

DR. LIVINGSTON: Oh, me too. Me too.

AUTHOR: Before I ask you any questions, I want to verify your request. You wa—

DR. LIVINGSTON: Oh yes, I want no editing of the interview please.

AUTHOR: Not a problem. You let me know as we go along if, for any reason, you say something that you change your mind about.

DR. LIVINGSTON: Right. I doubt that. That would make me a hypocrite.

---

1 Conducted via video/audio chat 10.10.2132. After further correspondence with Dr. Livingston, I was given permission to remove all fillers (e.g. um, uh, er). Current form approved by Dr. Livingston 10.12.2133.

AUTHOR: *(laughs)* If you say so. *(pause)* Dr. Livingston, let me start by asking you what you think the Angel Paradigm is?

DR. LIVINGSTON: Hah, you're starting with the hardest one! Well first off, I don't think the Angel Paradigm is just one idea—it's a lot of ideas put together. But a simple way to think of it is robots are humanity's guardian angels. That's where the name came from, isn't it? This fundamentally changes the relationship between humans and robots.

AUTHOR: How so?

DR. LIVINGSTON: Well, they started as tools, really. In reality they still are, but with the Angel Paradigm they are given a type of power. This tends to be a big deal for people, as these tools are suddenly exerting some level of control over their masters.

AUTHOR: But the humans are still the masters.

DR. LIVINGSTON: Of course. And we are talking about guardian angels here, not overlords. But humans have an innate desire to be in control of their lives.

AUTHOR: Would you say humans aren't in control?

DR. LIVINGSTON: That's a very difficult question to answer. What is control, really? With the Paradigm, it's all about dependency. The more we depend on robots, the more they are in control. Some of this dependency can be alarming, to some people. For example, what about teachers? A robot teaching humans in an academic system is in direct control of that human's intellectual development. Now in my opinion that's quite a bit of power. I'm not afraid of it, but I recognize it.

AUTHOR: Isn't the usual argument that the humans program the teaching, so the humans are still in control?

DR. LIVINGSTON: Right, which makes this relationship even more fascinating. Robots are just tools, but they have been given an aura of control by the Paradigm.

AUTHOR: Do you think the level of control will change with time?

DR. LIVINGSTON: Yes, absolutely. I think the Paradigm is always evolving, and each step of the way, the general public gets anxious. Now that isn't meant to put them down, I'm pretty much on the same boat. When I hear about putting robots in the legislature or the judiciary, it can get concerning. And again this is all about dependency. The reason the level of control will increase is because the level of dependency will increase.

AUTHOR: Do you think artificial love is related to this dependency?

DR. LIVINGSTON: Now there's the question I was waiting for! Yes, absolutely. AL blurs the line of what it means to be human, and how—sacred?—emotions are.

AUTHOR: How does artificial love relate to the Angel Paradigm?

DR. LIVINGSTON: Because of the type of dependency. Compare our two examples, AL and the robot legislature. The robot legislature is programmed and controlled by humans, but we still have a logical opposition to it. AL can be— well, I've heard it called more 'sinister.' Basically a robot seducing a human, in the emotional sense. With the legislature, we feel like we can fight that control, but not with AL. AL is toying with our emotions. Some people really do fall in love with robots or computers.

AUTHOR: When did AL start?

DR. LIVINGSTON: Before the Revolution, although those were usually unique cases. Social outcasts and the like. It was a big concern during the Revolution but remember most of the new robots were laborers. There was a small surge in cases around the end of the 2100s. That's when the social recalibration programs came around, with mixed success.[2] Really it's still an issue today: is it right, is it moral, etcetera. Again we're talking about AL, an emotional connection—physical relationships with robots are something different, but they can overlap with AL. If you look at physical relationships with robots, the numbers are much higher. But that's a whole other issue.

AUTHOR: Is AL—emotional AL—growing significantly? I guess specifically do you think it represents a big part of the Paradigm, or that it might in the future?

DR. LIVINGSTON: The numbers I'm aware of have been stable for the past decade at least. Now for a lot of people there is still a lot of stigma associated with these relationships, or they might not believe they are in love with a robot but they are, or they might even have a functional human relationship but a robot one on the side. It can get pretty complicated. But in terms of the Paradigm, well, you also can't see it as black and white. I mean when does emotional attachment reach love? I don't think you can answer that question with humans, let alone humans

[2] After the Robotic Revolution and during the labor crisis, there was an uptick in cases of human/computer and human/robot relationships. Some governments, such as in the United States and Japan, began what were known as 'social recalibration programs' in order to discourage these sorts of relationships and encourage human/human relationships. This was widely seen as a knee-jerk reaction to the Revolution. In this case, the surge in 'artificial' relationships was seen as a potential beginning to a problem that could grow out of control, hence the recalibration efforts.

and robots. And many people are at least lightly attached to their robots. Surely you've heard of emotional manipulation by robots. Certain models were able to emulate sadness or guilt, and used it as a bargaining tool with their masters, much like a dog might beg for a treat. This was definitely something that scared a lot of people, robots being able to fool us into doing what they wanted. Thankfully most of our current models are focused on jobs that involve little to no emotional articulation, but there is still that shadow of possibility. Between that and everything else we've discussed, you start to see a web of dependency, some emotional, some physical, some parts stronger, some parts weaker—that's the Paradigm. And I think it's only going to get bigger.

AUTHOR: Going back to the idea of an evolving Paradigm, how do you feel independent morality could impact the situation?

DR. LIVINGSTON: That's a good question. With independent morality, at least held to some sort of test or standard, many positions that are currently off-limits to robots would theoretically open. But do we want those to open? This is really the bridge that can take us to a true robotic judiciary. Personally speaking, that sounds like a bad idea. I get all of the positives, but it comes down to what we mean by independent morality. I just don't think morality on a human scale is possible in the near future, or even ever. How do you program that? I don't know.

AUTHOR: But assuming it is programmed, how will this affect the web of control?

DR. LIVINGSTON: Yes, sorry. With independent morality, robots have the potential to increase their level of control and by extension our level of dependency. As with all our other examples, this will clash with our human desires. In the long run, however, I think the convenience of robot control, and the promise of a leisure society, will put robots into positions of more and more power. But that's in the long run. Then again, if you look at where we are today versus where we were thirty years ago, you'd be surprised by how much we've let robots control our lives. What we consider normal changes every day.

AUTHOR: Can you talk a little about the relationship between robot morality and religion?

DR. LIVINGSTON: Sure. Many religions hold that humans are unique, special, that we have a soul or a spirit. This is— and they say robots cannot. And since our morality comes from this spirit, a robot can never truly be moral. Now I take it we are segueing toward the Paradigm and its religious implications?

AUTHOR: Yes, please continue.

DR. LIVINGSTON: Yes, so the easiest analogy is right there in the name, and I said it at the beginning—robots are human's guardian angels. Of course, this tends to disagree with many of the older religions, to the point of blasphemy, but there is also Robotism.[3] Only a few thousand people call themselves members, but it's still a religion. What's so interesting about it in terms of our conversation is they take the Angel Paradigm literally, and that opens up a whole new set of questions. First of all, could this religion be bereft of faith? Or, what I mean to say is, well— it's hard to talk about this without being offensive to typical religions, but we can agree that those tend to come with a fair share of skeptics. But

[3] Robotism is covered in more detail by Pastor Lem (chapter 10).

Robotism is, in a way, the Angel Paradigm, which as we keep saying, is becoming more and more prominent. For lack of a better way of putting it, it's a religion that's coming true before our eyes. Again, I don't mean offense I just don't know a better way of saying it.

AUTHOR: Don't worry, none taken.

DR. LIVINGSTON: Thanks, but it's not you I'm worried about! *(laughs)* Anyways, Robotism is definitely a bit beyond our current reality, and some followers think of robots as the ancient type of angels—as their god's gift to man, the path to peace, enlightenment, whatever it might be. This puts a spiritual value on robots that's separate from any value ever held by computers alone. It's really quite fascinating. But what was I—right, so, with this spiritual value, robots really become more like guardian angels. A lot of people shun the idea of robots being in control, but others don't think of it as control. I mean, do angels control? The more accepted idea in these Robotist circles is that the robots guide us, again towards enlightenment or whatever the case may be, but that humans retain the control—humans remain special and superior. That's much easier for our pride to swallow. Now if you ask me, there is a lot of overlap between guidance and control, and guidance and dependency, which brings us back to our earlier discussion. But to each their own. At least they accept it willingly.

AUTHOR: Is it all black and white? You seem to be saying that Robotism embraces the rise of the Paradigm and other religions reject it.

DR. LIVINGSTON: Oh, that was not my intention, of course there is a spectrum of acceptance. Different individuals and groups within different religions have their own ideas of robots and the Paradigm. The idea that robots are humanity's path to peace is not unique to Robotism. Notably, some forms of Islam and Christianity support this message. They do not place too much spiritual value on the robots, but they recognize their importance.

AUTHOR: Do you think the development of independent morality will change the way religions treat robots? Or— and I know this is far-fetched and— but what if robots gain a consciousness?

DR. LIVINGSTON: Ha, well, the answer to both of those questions is yes, of course their position will change. The real question is how. Let's start with the more possible scenario: independent morality. Sticking to a strictly religious perspective, this will only add fuel to the fire about what is and isn't moral. I mean, think about the people that have to program these things—who makes the choices? If a given robot aligns with the moral values of a given religion, there might be some level of acceptance. Even then, the key word is 'might.' For most religions, a robot with independent morality is too close to a human to be natural or acceptable. Even as an atheist, I don't think robots should have access to moral decisions involving humans. Now the consciousness situation is much more complicated. Assuming it ever reaches the point where a robot has a conscience—and further assuming we are able to define what it means to have a conscience, which is a whole different problem altogether—we will see a massive shift in society, not just religion. Are they equal to humans, do they have the same rights, how much do we control in terms of programming them versus now teaching them like humans—you get the point. And religions would have to decide these things, especially if they are equal or at least different but equal to humans. It might be a wild claim, but I'm sure some religions would agree that with a conscience comes a soul. Now there's something to think about!

AUTHOR: We talked a bit earlier about how independent morality might impact the Paradigm. What about consciousness?

DR. LIVINGSTON: I think robot consciousness would totally change the Paradigm, far more than independent morality or any other development. If robots gain consciousness, they become more human, and this changes our idea of dependency. We might not like the idea of cold machines making decisions for us, but what about machines with our own flaws? In some circles, the Paradigm is seen as freedom from human corruption, but if robots become human-like, will we have robot corruption instead? This is known as the anthropomorphic paradox, and it's a very complicated problem. Once robots reach a certain level of 'humanness,' what sort of surprises might come up? Not to mention the alarmist theories involving robot takeovers.

AUTHOR: If I may diverge for a moment—

DR. LIVINGSTON: Certainly.

AUTHOR: How do you feel about these theories?

DR. LIVINGSTON: Of robot takeover?

AUTHOR: Or rebellion, yes.

DR. LIVINGSTON: Well I think I feel the way any scientist should feel—I don't know. I can make educated guesses about robots with a grasp of morality, but robots with self-awareness are the realm of science fiction, in my opinion. I don't know what might happen with a robot consciousness, but I can say one thing is certain: it will not happen overnight. And I don't mean on a timeline, I mean the consciousness itself.

Robots won't go from zero consciousness to human. There will be a middle ground— the best analogy is animals. I just hope we recognize it when it happens.

AUTHOR: Going back to your specialty of AL, do you think if robots reach consciousness, that it can still rightfully be called artificial?

DR. LIVINGSTON: Wow, you wouldn't believe how often I've thought about this. Then again, I have some qualms with the term 'artificial' now. For many people, there is nothing artificial about their love for a robot. Is your love for a pet artificial because it isn't human? Yes, a pet is an animal, so is love defined between animals alone? Some people would say yes but humans aren't that simple. We can feel love in many ways for many things. But no, I don't think it can rightfully be called artificial, even now. There's an equal amount of artificiality in millions of human relationships, but we don't abbreviate that as AL.

AUTHOR: *(laughs)* Very true. *(pause)* So in the end, you believe this depends on the definition of love, which is itself hard to define?

DR. LIVINGSTON: Exactly. That's what makes my work and research rather complicated. What is love? Certainly not a question I can claim to answer. There has been some fascinating work by cognitive scientists and neuroscientists, testing brain and body responses of humans to robots they share an emotional or physical relationship with. Long story short, while it might be called AL, the same chemicals are being released and the same neurons are firing. How artificial can that be?

AUTHOR: I'd like to branch into a more historical perspective…

DR. LIVINGSTON: Of course.

AUTHOR: …and ask you about the belief in the Paradigm before, during, and after the Initiative.

DR. LIVINGSTON: Ah yes. This is a great topic. The Paradigm emerged as a large scale public concept with the passage of the Fair Care Act. Although it was—what was it? I think sixteen—yes, sixteen years after the start of the Revolution, the Act filled two requirements: one, it was seen as a major positive step in society; and two, it was seen as almost entirely thanks to robotics. The Revolution itself was a major step, but at first glance, a negative one. The labor crisis shrouded the future in mystery and fear. But with the Fair Care Act, it was as if the whole idea of robotics was flipped on its head. Now they were making life easier, healthier. This brought the Paradigm into play. This changed the public opinion. From the Paradigm came the Initiative, and somewhere in this formative process, Michael Trualt and the Initiators entered the scene. Now when you say during the Initiative, do you mean between the override and the Initiative itself?

AUTHOR: Yes.

DR. LIVINGSTON: Right, well, that was the true test of the Paradigm, and thanks to some fantastic propaganda, it passed. For over a decade, people in the United States and several other countries had experienced nearly free, top of the line healthcare due to robotics. It wasn't difficult to convince them that robots had much more to offer, and society as a whole could function under their umbrella. What *was* difficult was dealing with our aforementioned web of control—the more the robots helped, the more the public saw the control. Of course, that see-saw continues today, and I think we are starting to reach the tipping point.

Every day you hear about some new law tightening the grip on robotics, a sort of reverse of the trend… but we'll get there in a second. I have a few more things to say about the period after the override. First off, the Initiators promised a future without worry. Healthcare was just the beginning, soon jobs would be out the window and people could do as they please! At this point, everything the robots did or would do in the future wasn't seen as control, but as service. The robots would do our bidding. But there's a fine line where that service evolves into control, and that's what's been happening in the years since the Initiative. After all, it's been more than four years, why do I still have to do a job? Clearly from me to you that's a ridiculous question, but for many people, the euphoria from the propaganda of the Initiators has created unrealistic expectations. So where does that leave the Paradigm? Well, honestly, it's like we discussed at the beginning: it's only growing stronger. But that doesn't stop the fact we are trying to slow it down—the public is growing more afraid than content. It won't matter, it's too late to put on the brakes now, but we'll try all the same.

AUTHOR: Do you think we have made— that we have passed a point of no return, so to speak?

DR. LIVINGSTON: Yes. Definitely. With the advances made in the robotics industry, we're not going to stop now. Limitations, legislative or otherwise, will fall in the face of innovation, for better or worse. We're lucky that the Initiative came about when it did and set the course of robotics in such a humanitarian direction, but even that may change in the coming years. Nothing is set in stone.

AUTHOR: How does that affect the Paradigm?

DR. LIVINGSTON: What exactly?

AUTHOR: If the humanitarian part of robotics fades.

DR. LIVINGSTON: Ah, well, you know as well as I do that that would fundamentally undermine the entire idea of the Paradigm. As it stands, the Paradigm calls for a positive effect by robots upon humanity. And not just as technological advancements, but as cultural and social advancements as well. In most definitions of the Paradigm, humanity reaches a new level of peace and cooperation. If robotics starts to focus on technological utility alone, there will continue to be socio-cultural side-effects, mainly because of its enormous influence, but it won't be the same. Worse, if we start to see robotics head in a more negative direction —for example, back to its military origins—well then we are in trouble. *(pause)* Yeah, honestly if you stop and think about it we are extremely lucky to have come out of the Initiative the way we did. I don't want to get into any argument about Trualt, but I will say I am glad things worked out the way they did.

AUTHOR: I know you just said you don't want to talk about Trualt--

DR. LIVINGSTON: Uh oh. *(laughs)* I knew this was coming!

AUTHOR: It was inevitable. But what do you see as Trualt's relationship with robotics and the Paradigm?

DR. LIVINGSTON: Trualt is a fascinating character, mostly due to his strict interpretation of the Paradigm, especially with the Robotic Assembly. That, more than anything, proves his view of the Paradigm, in the same way his part in the override and Initiative proves his contribution to the Paradigm. The robotic legislature is such a radical idea today, and the fact he was thinking about it six or seven years ago—that's fascinating. As I said, I completely disagree, but it's still fascinating.

AUTHOR: You've mentioned multiple times you don't think robotics will reach a point where the robot legislature or judiciary is possible, correct?

DR. LIVINGSTON: In my opinion, no, they will not, correct.

AUTHOR: Then do you think there's a ceiling to the Paradigm? A line it will never cross?

DR. LIVINGSTON: Yes, I do. And you know what, I might be wrong. Honestly, seeing the advances in robotics going on around us, I'm starting to doubt myself. By the time this interview is printed, I might even have changed my mind. But as of now, I still believe that true robot morality is not possible, and even if it is, we will run into the anthropomorphic paradox well before we can actually have the robots run the government. So yes, I think there is a ceiling to the Paradigm, a point where their web of control ends. This is a good thing though, since it means we can remain an independent species, at least in some small way.

AUTHOR: That is a great topic, can you talk about the Paradigm and human independence as a species?

DR. LIVINGSTON: Sure, but it's the same thing we've been talking about. Again, us humans, we use tools, we make things easier for ourselves through our intelligence. But when a hammer becomes a car becomes a robot doctor, are we still in control of our lives? You might be asking the wrong person, I'm a psychologist, not a philosopher… *(laughs)*

AUTHOR: One more subject Dr. Livingston, if I may.

DR. LIVINGSTON: Of course.

AUTHOR: How do you feel biorobotics impacts the Paradigm? I know that's a bit vague—

DR. LIVINGSTON: No, no, that's a big question, an important question. And often overlooked. After all, the majority of robots are strictly mechanical. I have to say it's a field that interests me very much, and I actually delve into a bit of these things in my upcoming book on AL. Anyways, I can split biorobotics into two main segments: making humans more robotic and making robots more human. Both of these, of course, have an impact on the Paradigm. Let's start with the first one. Robotic modification of humans has progressed an incredible amount since the Revolution. However, this is a field where the term 'robot' and 'robotic' is still a bit clouded. You see, robot now refers almost exclusively to an electromechanical entity capable of independent reasoning. In most cases, it's also assumed to be humanoid, although there's some wiggle room there. But the point is electromechanical replacements, such as an arm or a kidney, have little to no independent reasoning ability. In this regard, they cannot truly be robotic, but they're still positive changes to the human condition brought about by robotics—a key part of the Paradigm. But what about BCIs?[4] BCIs have been around for over a hundred years, and they have evolved into a fascinating market. Blindness, deafness, and paralysis are, for the most part, afflictions of the past. In most cases, a BCI lacks any reasoning capability, and falls under the same category as the arm or the organ. Still, even if these are not strictly robotic modifications, they are worth understanding. Especially when you cross

[4] Brain-Computer Interfaces

the line from replacement to enhancement. What about switching out your arms for a set of super-strong robot arms? This has, for now, been severely limited by the rest of the body, but they exist to some extent. What's gaining more ground are BCIs for brain enhancement. Now, you might even have some primitive attempt at boosting a human brain's abilities through a BCI, does this mean the BCI is reasoning? No, but this is still a monumental change for humanity. After all, these are essentially cyborgs. Now, there is a growing number of roboticists and other scientists who see a potential future where the path of these cyborgs continues to a point where humanity and robots merge, but I am not sure about that. Even now, such modifications are seen as bizarre or unnecessary in most cases.[5] Of course, if we ever end up going down that path, it would throw the Angel Paradigm as we know it out of the window. Now let me rewind here, I still have to talk about the other part, robots becoming more human, right?

AUTHOR: Yes please.

DR. LIVINGSTON: Of course. This will all lead back to the same conversation anyways. So that side of biorobotics is, from my perspective, more closely associated with the Angel Paradigm. The most famous example here would be the android, or a robot that resembles a human down to the most minute detail—or at least externally. This has proven a more complicated problem than originally thought, but great advances have been made in the field. Really, there are a few obstacles that prevent the widespread use of androids. There is, of course, the uncanny valley,

---

[5] Cyborgs are covered in more detail by Ms. Marotto (chapter 13).

although that is a very complex issue.[6] It mostly boils down to two things: one, a moral opposition, and two, a lack of purpose. The moral opposition is clear enough: robots that look or behave like humans are an abomination to some, and frightening to others. But the lack of purpose is more important. What use does a truly humanoid robot have? These robots are unfit for most robotic labor, and they become more of a novelty. There is, of course, the pornographic business, and it alone drives a good 90% of the android market, but beyond that, not much else. My own research deals with androids very frequently, both in the pornographic sector and of course with AL, and then how humans react to androids, and so on. Originally it was thought robots resembling humans would impart comfort on others, but here the uncanny valley can come into play. Even if the android is sophisticated enough to fool us physically, it will not be able to fool us very long with its speech patterns. At least not yet. And then of course there are mannerisms, gestures, and all the subtle things that make us human that are driving many current research ventures. The point is, androids could change the dynamic of the Angel Paradigm. While most robots are humanoid—that was kind of the whole idea of the Revolution—they are still mostly metallic and mechanical. If, somehow, androids caught on, how would that change our outlook on all that dependency we talked about earlier? Here again, my own research and the research of my colleagues can shed some light on

---

[6] The uncanny valley refers to the idea that at a certain point of 'humanness' an android will actually be repulsive, because of the minor inconsistencies between the android and a true human. For example, a typical metallic robot is less repulsive than an android with clearly plastic skin and eyes that don't blink.

the issue. At this time, the evidence suggests that the uncanny valley is an individualized spectrum. For some people, more or less human-like robots can cause more or less discomfort. However, for— well, I need to check my notes since you are quoting me, hold on… *(long pause)* Sorry!

AUTHOR: Not a problem.

DR. LIVINGSTON: Right, so, for 92% of subjects, physical human characteristics beyond shape cause discomfort. This includes things like fake skin, hair, clothing, whatever. This finding ties directly to the Paradigm, because humans will avoid dependence on robots that cause discomfort. Therefore, a wider usage of androids will lessen the strength of the Paradigm. Of course, no one can say for certain if things won't change. Perhaps acceptance will increase, and discomfort will wane. But as of now, androids are a detriment to the Paradigm. You can see the same discomfort with robotic dogs and other pets, although that has little bearing on thc Paradigm. Again, I don't mean the metallic kind, I mean the kind that are physically mimicking animals in things like fur or eyelids. Now all of this goes under the umbrella of what I like to call 'external biorobotics' as opposed to 'internal biorobotics,' which is a much smaller field. This is where you see things like robots with internal organic components. Most of these are experiments or ventures of discovery, as they have yet to find much use for such things. But they exist. Sorry I'm getting a bit lost here, there's a lot to say.

AUTHOR: No problem.

DR. LIVINGSTON: Okay, so, thinking about the androids again, or just the idea of robots becoming more like humans, you come back to what we mentioned earlier: the path of humans and robots merging. If you have robots becoming more like humans and humans becoming more like robots, will there eventually be a point where we cross a sort of fifty-fifty line? Well, if there ever is, you can really get into the philosophical stuff like what it means to be human. For example, what about a robot with a human's brain? This is so far beyond current technology it's a bit silly to ask but that would surely change our way of life. I don't even know what that would do with the Angel Paradigm but it would definitely be different than it is now! Actually, there is one more topic I'd like to cover, if that's alright?

AUTHOR: Of course.

DR. LIVINGSTON: Thank you. Biorobotics and the merging of humans and robots reminded me of transhumanism, which is closely related. Just to give a quick primer, transhumanism is the idea of altering the human condition via technology to make us more intelligent, more powerful, etc. So in a way, cyborgs are transhuman. But transhumanism also covers ideas such as life extension, the elimination of genders, proactive human evolution… all kinds of interesting, science fiction stuff that overlaps robotics and the Angel Paradigm in many ways. The reason I bring it up in the first place is the classic idea of the uploaded brain. If humans find a way to upload their consciousness to a computer, that will completely change the nature of, well, everything! Here we see the same questions about what it means to be human, but we also see an enticing possibility: can we create a simulated reality, maintained by robots, where humans are uploaded and live their lives digitally and happily, perhaps even immortally? Is this in line with the Angel Paradigm? I would say it isn't in the classic sense, but it is in a general sense. Anyways, that was a bit of a digression but I think it's a very fascinating subject. Not what I usually focus on, but it pertains to the Angel Paradigm. Okay *(laughs)* that's it, I'm done, I promise.

AUTHOR: Again, not a problem, your thoroughness is appreciated.

DR. LIVINGSTON: *(laughs)* Well, not by everyone.

AUTHOR: *(laughs)* No, the more in-depth, the better. In fact, we've discussed everything I hoped to cover and more.

DR. LIVINGSTON: Glad I could help.

AUTHOR: Thank you, Dr. Livingston—

DR. LIVINGSTON: Of course!

AUTHOR: —it's been a pleasure speaking with you.

DR. LIVINGSTON: Likewise. Thank you for having me. And good luck with your book!

AUTHOR: Thank you. I will contact you soon about the transcription.

DR. LIVINGSTON: I look forward to hearing from you. Take care.

4. Eduardo Santola, Lawyer - - Edited Interview[1]

Mr. Santola was the prosecuting attorney in Rivera Corporation v United Robotics, the retroactively precedent-setting case of robot motive.[2] *He remains a popular and influential attorney in Buenos Aires.*

In most cases, the Angel Paradigm is touted as a solution to humanity's problems, but this is not the truth. From my perspective, from what I have been a part of, I understand this cannot be the case. While many disagree with my position, most do so without understanding my views. I hope I can present a clear picture of what, in my opinion, many people have decided to simply ignore.

Robotics is by many measures the most volatile legal field in history. The unprecedented evolution of the technology makes numerous laws outdated before they have even been agreed upon. The legal status of robots is a hotbed of divisive issues, and I'd like to address as many of these as possible. After all, it's important to understand the Angel Paradigm from a legal standpoint, both now and in the future. I don't doubt that by the time my statements here are printed, the situation will have changed, but I will do my best to anticipate what I foresee happening. It's an inexact science, at best.

The first major robotic issue to affect the legal system was robots as witnesses. Within the first few years of this century, robots were everywhere, many with audio and video recording capabilities that were

---

[1] Conducted via video/audio chat 06.11.2133. Questions were translated from English to Spanish and answers were translated from Spanish to English by one robot. The same robot translated all edits sent to Mr. Santola for review. Current form approved by Mr. Santola 04.05.2134.

[2] When the Earth Court was established, it took on official precedents from many noteworthy cases from around the world. *Rivera Corporation v United Robotics* currently defines most legal understandings of robot intent. This account details the differences in the legal definitions of motive and intent, but I have left the word motive above as it corresponds to the general public's understanding.

used as evidence in countless criminal cases. This led to a few interesting situations, most famous of which was the Frémont case.

In 2100, Dr. Jean-François Frémont, a noted French roboticist at the time, was arrested for tampering with robotic evidence in connection with dozens of high-profile criminal investigations, often leading to improper verdicts in favor of the highest bidder. Frémont was in a unique position as a judiciary expert on robots, and was ironically tasked with investigating robot data for potential manipulation. Robot software was and is rather secure, but as with any technology, humans always make the weakest link. Frémont and his colleagues were usually able to detect any sort of manipulation, but if Frémont himself was adding the finishing touches, no one would notice.

After a series of videos disappeared, and thanks to some aggressively inquisitive prosecutors, Frémont was caught by one of his co-workers. The media warned the public that robots were unreliable as witnesses while roboticists underlined the human element. In this case, the media was right. Evidence is not measured by its intention, but by its presentation. Even if humans caused the problem, there was still a problem with robots as witnesses. This debate would continue up until the creation of the cerebral unit, which prevented all but the most sophisticated level of tampering and solidified robotic evidence once more. Currently, robot testimony is one of the most robust forms of evidence in the justice system and is often considered unquestionable. This is, in my opinion, a grave error, and seems to show that we have learned nothing from the Frémont case. There are still many ways humans can interact or interfere with robots, and there are just as many people with influence who would aim to cause such interference.

Besides the Frémont case, the main issue arising from robot audio and video recording was privacy. Even the earliest models were able to hold many days of audio and video data, and no standards of privacy existed yet. Most countries had to pass legislation on the availability and use of robot data, and intelligence agencies eagerly met with robot manufacturers for possible access to certain models' stored information.

Such major issues weren't the only examples of privacy affairs spurred by robot surveillance. Many police departments and some neighborhoods instituted a robot watch program, leaving a robot or more to patrol the streets. The old security versus liberty debate had a new face, and many concessions were made to appease privacy advocates. While the true extent of NSA or GCHQ access may never be known, there were certainly great strides made in robotic data security research in these years. The issue was effectively laid to rest by a combination of the cerebral unit, cerebral scanning, and the Earth Initiative, although many people believe the remnants of national intelligence agencies have found a way to hack this data. Of course, there was Trualt's infamous software within the Athena, but robotics companies insist this is now impossible.

The next major robotic legal issue—by far the most famous—would be murder by robot. Only one year after the Frémont case, in 2101, Dr. Jeremy Skellar managed to murder another human being with a civilian robot despite the supposedly extreme number of preventative measures within the machines. Before the Skellar case, there were 107 reported human deaths by civilian humanoid robots, all ruled accidental. To this day, the Skellar case remains the only successful murder of a human by a civilian robot,[3] although there have been thousands of injuries and nearly a thousand more accidental deaths.

Like Frémont, Skellar was also a famous roboticist, one of McRay's most coveted research scientists. Unfortunately, his expertise allowed him to remove significant portions of a Benjamin model's software and install his own creation, a near exact copy of the original operating system that was missing the critical portion preventing direct human harm. Upon further investigation, many roboticists found his work to be absolutely

[3] This is assuming a robot of high enough intelligence to understand that it is hurting a human being.

brilliant, although completely unethical. The number of work-arounds in his alteration confounded scientists with their complexity and ingenuity; Skellar was able to have his personal Benjamin change without any problems. The creation of the software was fueled by knowledge of his wife's infidelity that ultimately led to his order to murder her lover. Skellar expected a clean escape, but even with his incredible modifications, after killing the man, the robot shut down. McRay received an automated shutdown notice with a flag for human harm and was given a warrant to access the robot's audio and video data, which showed Skellar's order and the robot's subsequent murder. Presently, cerebral scanning and the Bureau of Robotic Affairs (BRA) act as a safeguard against such sophisticated tampering.

Skellar was charged with first-degree murder, initiating a small debate on his level of culpability. For most, a robot was equivalent to a gun, a tool that could harm but had no motive of its own. This was the proper verdict at the time, but the issue of robot motive would evolve along with their intelligence.

When examining these definitions, it is important to understand the legal distinction between motive and intent. Motive is the cause that induces a certain action, whereas intent is the decision to bring about a consequence. For example, if one man stabs another, then there is intent to harm, but the motive is (as of yet) unknown. With robots, each of these variables presents a challenge. Clearly, if a human asks a robot to perform an action, the human has the intent but the robot has the motive (the human intends that the action take place, the robot is programmed to follow the command). This simple scenario puts culpability on the human, and leads directly to the Skellar ruling.

But what about autonomous actions? Even the Benjamin was capable of a wide range of self-directed actions and a certain amount of learning, and robot intelligence has grown exponentially since then. Then, if a robot is shown to have motive and intent, do they qualify as defendants, or are their manufacturers responsible?

Many scenarios are listed in robotic law books, and not all of them have a clear answer. A common type of hypothetical is a robot savior: for example, if a robot runs in front of a moving car to save a pedestrian, who is responsible for the damages to the car? More serious examples occur in the medical field: what if a robot fails to identify a symptom, sign, or situation that leads to improper treatment, injury, or even death? Is the robot responsible?

In most cases, the applicable human laws, such as good samaritan clauses, have been expanded to include robots. And again in most cases, if the robot is found responsible, then really the manufacturer is responsible.

The issue of robot motive and intent culminated in 2123 with the Rivera case. The Rivera Corporation was a multinational healthcare conglomerate that ran several hospitals across South America. Rivera had over a million robots operating as doctors, nurses, and various low-level administrators.

In 2122, the Hospital Rivera de Buenos Aires was one of the most prominent hospitals in the Rivera system, and the most frequented in all of Argentina. The hospital had sixteen surgical robots, fourteen of which where new Aurora models manufactured by United Robotics. These robots were the first to include cerebral units and cerebral scanning. In 2122, cerebral scanning was still a new technology, and the BRA did not yet exist. When an Aurora model detected a change in another Aurora model's code, it would trigger an automatic remote shut-down of the affected robot. If this didn't work, the data was sent to UR for immediate review and action.

Generally, there were two reasons a remote shut-down would not work. Either there were modifications made to the remote shut-down system (extremely difficult, but possible), or the remote shut-down was disabled due to UR's original programming. This was only in the event that the robot in question was in the process of preventing a human from coming to harm. In other words, if a robot was, for example, saving a human from drowning when another robot detected that its code had been tampered with, the robot would not be shut-down remotely. Instead, the information would be flagged and sent to UR, and the robot would be allowed to continue saving the human from drowning.

In the Hospital Rivera de Buenos Aires, the surgery robots were used almost non-stop year-round. There was enough break provided for daily maintenance and checks, but otherwise all fourteen Aurora surgery models were performing an average of 12 surgeries per day.[4] During a routine maintenance procedure on June 4th, 2122, the Aurora model code-named Surgeon 4 was compromised by a staff roboticist. The Aurora code was illegally accessed and modified to direct Surgeon 4 to divulge certain privileged information regarding patients of the hospital. Most of the robots in the hospital were able to access all patient records for efficiency purposes, and the roboticist in question was selling patient information to interested parties.

The malicious code was inserted at 14:27. At 15:33, another Aurora surgery robot, Surgeon 11, performed a cerebral scan of Surgeon 4 and detected the modification. At the time, however, Surgeon 4 was in surgery, so a remote shut-down was not activated (as this would lead to human harm). In this scenario, Surgeon 11 was programmed to send the data to UR, but it did not. Surgeon 11 experienced an irresolvable logical conflict and went catatonic at 15:34. This self-shut-down occurred mid-surgery, and caused severe injury to the patient, though she survived. At 16:12, another Aurora model (a non-surgical hospital robot) detected Surgeon 4's modification and sent the data to UR.

At 16:15, UR sent a roboticist to examine and retrieve Surgeon 4, and contacted the hospital to let them know. It was then that they learned of the malfunction with Surgeon 11. This set off a series of events that would lead to the eventual case against UR. UR immediately sent a whole team of roboticists to retrieve both robots, but the hospital did not want

[4] Data provided as evidence in *Rivera Corporation v United Robotics* for January 1st, 2122 to June 3rd, 2122.

to let them take Surgeon 11. Instead, they insisted that an independent agency examine the robot. However, Rivera's contract with UR stipulated that after a self-shut-down, the affected model would immediately fall under UR jurisdiction. At 16:58, the UR team arrived, and by 17:15, they had left with both Surgeon 4 and Surgeon 11. Rivera continued to contact UR and the police, asking that UR provide the police and the hospital with the data retrieved from Surgeon 11, but UR refused.

The next day, the affected patient filed a malpractice suit against the hospital. Rivera immediately filed a motion to dismiss, claiming UR was liable for Surgeon 11's malfunction. In their contract with UR, Rivera was responsible for regular and appropriate maintenance of the robots, but UR was liable for any malfunctions unrelated to Rivera interference. The court was able to examine the maintenance logs and agreed that Rivera had upheld its responsibilities as the owners, and as per their contract with UR, they were not liable for the damages to the patient. The motion to dismiss was granted.

However, the incident was receiving a significant amount of negative press, and when UR divulged the modifications made to Surgeon 4, the focus shifted to the culpability of the staff member who inserted the malicious code, but with UR still refusing to comment on Surgeon 11—and therefore neither confirming nor denying its malfunction's relationship to Surgeon 4 and the malicious code—the hospital reasoned the malfunction must be UR's responsibility. The following day, the Rivera Corporation filed a lawsuit against United Robotics for breach of contract and hired me as prosecuting attorney.

The trial itself lasted over four months, but I will focus on the important points. Other sources give much more detailed accounts. UR was instructed to reveal the code for Surgeon 11 at the time of failure. Several roboticists, mostly from UR and some independent, testified on the meaning of the code. The consensus reached by these roboticists led to an entirely new legal challenge.

According to the roboticists, when Surgeon 11 first ran the cerebral scan and detected the modifications in Surgeon 4 during Surgeon 4's surgery, it was presented with the command to send the information to UR as per protocol. However, Surgeon 11 had noted that Surgeon 4 had hundreds of surgeries scheduled in the coming weeks. Surgeon 11 knew that if it reported Surgeon 4, Surgeon 4 would be pulled off-duty. Due to the immense demand for surgery at the time, Surgeon 11 reasoned that the other robots, itself included, would not be capable of fulfilling Surgeon 4's duties, and the patients would go without surgery. Therefore, it decided not to report the modification, as it seemed to lead to human harm. This represented an unprecedented level of reasoning, surpassing a highly prioritized command line, but this was not the end of the situation.

Surgeon 11 further reasoned that another robot would eventually scan Surgeon 4 and detect the modification. To this end, it decided that the other Aurora models's cerebral scanning capability would need to be disabled. However, code modifications had to be done physically; they could not be performed wirelessly. Because cerebral scans happen constantly and randomly, Surgeon 11 reasoned that it needed to rendezvous with each Aurora model immediately in order to prevent Surgeon 4's deactivation (again reasoning that this would allow humans to come to harm). However, Surgeon 11 was busy performing its own surgery at the time, meaning that leaving its post would allow a human to come to harm. Faced with a decision between the human it was performing surgery on and the other humans it now felt responsible for, it reached an irresolvable logic conflict and went catatonic.

This outcome was peculiar. UR had many safety mechanisms in place to deal with potential conflicts of interest such as this one. For example, the choice between saving one life or three, or a child's life versus an adult's. This was basic ethical programming, highly controversial but necessary for exactly the type of situation that rendered Surgeon 11 inert. UR admitted that these decisions were simplified to mathematical models, essentially assigning a value of importance to one situation versus another.

Whichever value was higher would be prioritized. In this case, the value assignments continued to fluctuate from one side to the other in rapid succession. A combination of hundreds if not thousands of factors—including the proximity of the other robots to Surgeon 11, the point it had reached in the surgery, and the rapidly evolving future schedule of the other robots—made it impossible to prioritize one action over the other, as the value continued to jump back and forth with such frequency, the robot was unable to comprehend the proper course of action and shut down.

At this point, it was clear that UR's programming inadvertently led to the self-shut-down that injured the patient. However, what of Surgeon 11's decision to not notify UR of Surgeon 4's modification? The cerebral scanning code used the second-highest prioritization available, just under 'definite' human harm. Normally, even if potential human harm was detected, the notification would be sent because it was not definite human harm. Surgeon 11 made a distinction between potential human harm and eventual definite human harm, assuming if it notified UR, the human harm would certainly happen, just in the future. This line of thought, while somewhat flawed, was unprecedented. The Aurora, along with every major robotic central processing component at the time, was made to reason beyond its perceived boundaries, but this was unexpected.

In the trial, Surgeon 11's line of reasoning brought up an interesting argument from UR: the company's responsibility over their creations remains within the confines of the creations's anticipated programming, barring outside interference. In other words, UR argued that because Surgeon 11 had gone beyond regular programming, its actions were not their responsibility. Returning to our definitions of motive and intent, this meant that if a robot acts in a programmed way, it is UR's intent. However, if a robot acts in a non-programmed way, it is either someone else's intent (via code modification) or, in this case, the robot's intent.

In many ways, this was like opening Pandora's box. The trial was not a public affair, but if it had been, the reaction would have been very interesting. UR was openly admitting a type of robot intent, a new and possibly dangerous level of independence. UR argued that although their programming caused the self-shut-down via the logic conflict, Surgeon 11's intent originally led to the logic conflict. Therefore, UR argued that Surgeon 11 was itself responsible for its shut-down.

Rivera countered that the ability to reason to an extent beyond programming is not only expected but encouraged by UR. This meant that the decision of Surgeon 11 to not send the notification was an extension of the original programming, even as an original thought.

In the end, the court sided with Rivera. Robotics corporations are responsible for their creations within the boundaries of their regular programming, as well as any deviations that occur without outside interference unauthorized by the corporation itself. This meant that robots that displayed an independent intent were still the responsibility of their manufacturer. The burden on robotics corporations made certain that their pursuit of intelligent robots was made safely. UR's motion to appeal was denied.

The effects of this case are seen industry-wide. Robotics corporations have, in many cases, increased their security measures with regards to programming of decision-making and logical reasoning. UR's irresolvable logic conflict was fixed, commanding the robot to make a randomized decision in the case of hyper-frequent prioritization fluctuation.

The philosophical questions regarding robotics and intent derived from this case are also worth note, although I personally believe these questions are unfounded. Surgeon 11 did not cross a line from dependent to independent reasoning. It was still acting out its programming, although it was able to push the boundaries in a legally questionable way that coincidentally caused its own failure. Many argue independent reasoning had been around well before Surgeon 11, and others argue it has yet to occur. The problem lies in how to define independent reasoning, and I'm not sure a satisfactory answer can be given. It is clear to see robots are evolving daily, and their reasoning is evolving with them. However, as with the verdict in the Rivera case, I believe robotic reasoning is still a function of their programming, and not something to be labelled truly independent.

There are two further stages in the future of robotics that will have monumental impact on our society, and at least one of them may finally lead to a fully independent robot. These stages are independent morality and robotic consciousness. In my opinion, these two phenomena will come hand in hand, but most roboticists feel that is not the case. For my part, I do not see how independent morality, and also independent reasoning, can be possible without consciousness. All other actions, such as those by Surgeon 11, are simply extensions of original programming.

However, I will examine the two stages separately from a legal standpoint. Independent morality without consciousness leads to robots with moral intent and possibly motive. If a robot makes an unprogrammed moral decision, who is responsible? If we agree with the common consensus that actions such as Surgeon 11's are independent, then the Rivera ruling can probably be expanded to include moral decisions. In many ways, Surgeon 11's decision was based on certain moral elements, although these were programmed to be logically comprehensible. Therefore, I believe independent morality will still be within the liability of the manufacturer.

Consciousness, on the other hand, would change everything. Here, the legal ramifications depend on the nature of the consciousness. If it is clearly sub-human, there is no telling how the legal system will handle the inevitable variety of situations that will occur. This will likely have to be a case-by-case system. But if it is a human level of consciousness, then we begin to enter the realm of science fiction, and the questions shift to the nature of the robots themselves. Are robots given rights or are they slaves to our will? Will robots be defendants, or prosecutors? These robots, if they were to exist, would reason at a truly independent level. The question would be if they are equal, or perhaps superior, to humans.

I would now like to return to my original conclusion, that the Angel Paradigm cannot exist in its true sense. Everything that I have explained about the legal history of robotics points in this direction, even if it may be hard to see. The main reason for this is a desire for the opposite: we choose to believe the Paradigm is possible, so there is a confirmation bias, but the reality is right in front of us. Robots are tools, useful but potentially dangerous machines that run on a complicated series of commands. Humans are the creators, the writers of these commands, and as such exert ultimate control over their creations. This is why every legal precedent, even that of the Rivera case, placed responsibility in the hands of the manufacturers. This is also why the Angel Paradigm is not possible.

The Paradigm relies on a truly independent robot, one that can see what is best for humankind without the guidance of humankind. But a truly independent robot can only arise with a consciousness matching that of a human. And if such a robot arises, its judgement will be clouded in the same way a human's is. This is, in my opinion, the fundamental flaw in the Paradigm.

Truthfully, there exists a spectrum of versions of the Paradigm, and some are within the realm of possibility. But the populist understanding of the term remains the idyllic one, and this one is impossible.

5. Casey Mooden, Virologist - - Expanded Presentation[1]

Dr. Mooden is a leading virologist at the Earth Health Organization, where she is head of the neurovirology lab. Her expertise in nanorobotics and nanomedicine give her a unique perspective on a different side of the Angel Paradigm.

I think almost every person on this planet would agree with me if I said robots have been an extremely valuable asset in medicine. Healthcare science is always working on technology and techniques that promote and develop human health, and robots are the newest in a long line of tools used for this purpose, a line that extends into prehistory.

The origins of robots in medicine extend well before the Robotic Revolution, into the days where the word robot meant something very different than it does now. In the beginning, the most sophisticated robots available in medicine were surgical robots. But unlike their autonomous present-day counterparts, these early surgical robots were no more than highly specialized tools that allowed surgeons to operate via remote manipulation. Over the following decades, these machines increased in complexity, eventually reaching a small level of autonomy just before the Revolution.

This budding autonomy caught the interest and imagination of Seth McRay, who saw a major opportunity to expand his mechanical arm business. At the time, McRay made arms for a multitude of firms from the same foundation. Each specific build had different software and exchangeable tools that would allow the arm to perform its specific duties. McRay realized he could use the autonomous software and a new set of

[1] Adapted from her presentation *Robots & Antibiotic Resistance* at the annual Western Nanorobotics Conference (05.06.2132). Dr. Mooden has elaborated on certain details regarding the history of robots and healthcare, and simplified several sections regarding virology and nanorobotics. She has also tied her presentation more closely to the Angel Paradigm. Current form approved by Dr. Mooden 30.03.2134.

specialized medical tools on his existing base and have a medical robot arm on the market.

As we all know, over the next few years this thought process evolved into an entire humanoid base model with the same specialized, exchangeable tools and software. He named this creation Charlie, and the Robotic Revolution began.

In the first iteration of Charlie, 82 out of 256 builds were healthcare-related—just under a third. McRay himself was a strong proponent of robotic healthcare, although that was more out of a desire to see his business succeed than out of a philanthropic mantra such as the Angel Paradigm. While the two need not be mutually exclusive, his future political actions made his personal beliefs on the matter quite clear.[2] In any case, McRay's actions helped us get to where we are today, and where we are today is a lot closer to the Angel Paradigm.

Since the Revolution, robot healthcare has tied in with the Angel Paradigm by increasing access and lowering cost. But when robots first started invading hospitals at the turn of the century, they actually drove prices up: although most administrative duties were now taken care of, robots were a costly investment. Many hospitals or clinics overestimated their immediate potential and needed to cover the expense. There is also the commonly cited example of a patient being unwilling to have a robot diagnose or treat them, but this is an exaggeration. In reality, robots were typically sought out for their perceived mechanical precision, and they were always accompanied by human doctors and nurses, at least in the beginning. In any case, the price was at first astronomical.

As with most aspects of the Revolution, everything changed within the first decade. By 2110, many robots were able to perform the majority of a doctor or nurse's duties, given their immediate and intricate understanding

[2] Dr. Mooden is likely referring to McRay's vehement opposition of the Basic Income Expansion which indirectly led to the downfall of the company. However, Seth McRay was also a vocal opponent of many attempts to pass robotics-subsidized healthcare legislation in the United States, including the eventually successful Fair Care Act.

of all data gathered by peripheral machinery. Medical workers tended to work in tandem with the robots to alleviate the potential unease of patients, but combined with their administrative work and the now-prevalent use of robots in most healthcare manufacturing, daily operating costs plummeted. This was a golden age for corporate healthcare, but the general public soon caught on to the massive profits and unchanging price.

The Fair Care Act of 2112 put a huge dent in these practices,[3] though it wouldn't be until the Initiative that free, high-quality healthcare became standard worldwide. Even today there remain problematic pockets of lower-quality healthcare, typically tied with Initiative-resistance, but this is slowly being eradicated. The passage of the Fair Care Act is commonly cited as the beginning of the Paradigm itself, at least as a cultural concept up for discussion. Robots were now reshaping the landscape of society, and not in the negative way they had overturned the labor force. In summary, they were beginning to live up to their utopian potential.

In my opinion, this utopian potential of robot healthcare extends well beyond the free, high-quality healthcare we have today. Before I go on, I need to define three distinct types of care: curative care, palliative care, and preventive care. Curative care is treatment for an existing medical condition where a cure is considered achievable. Palliative care is treatment for an existing medical condition where a cure is not considered achievable. Preventive care consists of measures taken to prevent the need for either curative or palliative care.

Clearly, from an idealistic Angel Paradigm perspective, the ultimate goal of robots in medicine is to reach a point where preventive care is advanced enough to almost (if not completely) eliminate the need for palliative care and perhaps even curative care. But classic robots, as adept as they may be at all three forms of care right now, are not capable of

[3] The economic aspects of the Fair Care Act are covered in detail by Dr. Taylor (chapter 2).

reaching this point on their own. They need the help of their sometimes overlooked cousins: nanobots.

Nanobots have a history matching that of their humanoid counterparts, but they did not share in the sudden and extreme proliferation brought by the Revolution. There are no cerebral units of that size today, and I'm not sure there ever will be. In many ways, the field of nanorobotics is considered separate from robotics, particularly since the word robot has evolved to refer to the humanoid variety. But in terms of the Angel Paradigm, nanorobotics is just as crucial as robotics.

Medical use of nanobots is theoretically unlimited. There are countless ways in which nanobots are able to or would be able to revolutionize human medicine and care. The current focal point of medicinal nanorobotics is an all-encompassing set of medical nanobots, spread throughout the human body, monitoring and altering our health metrics (colloquially, these theoretical nanobots are known as medbots).

This is a lofty goal, and probably something left for the future, but we are closer than anyone would have anticipated even a few years ago. Currently, about 18% of the population has some form of medicinal nanobots in their systems. While this is quite a significant portion of the population (and the numbers continue to grow), there is a great deal of hesitation regarding medicinal nanotechnology. Concerns range from the rational (such as malfunctions, immune response, or network-based infiltration) to the paranoid (such as government tracking or targeted biological attacks).

Medbots may still be the realm of science fiction, but there are several important uses for medicinal nanobots today, with one in particular standing out: viral phage therapy, my own line of work. What is viral phage therapy? To better answer this question, let me explain the problem it was designed to solve: antibiotic resistance.

When antibiotics first began to take hold worldwide in the second half of the twentieth century, their overuse and misuse were the least of anyone's concerns—after all, they were saving lives. However, around the

2030s, antibiotic resistance became a global health threat. The layman's explanation is simple: the more an antibiotic is used to combat a certain microorganism, the more that microorganism tends to evolve resistance. After all, if we kill all the bacteria that an antibiotic can kill, the leftover bacteria are the ones we can't kill, and those are the ones that will reproduce (this is a gross simplification, but let's allow it).

Unfortunately, humans as a whole can be rather ignorant, and this basic premise was disregarded to a terrific degree in favor of easy fixes and quick profits. Antibiotics were overused in agriculture and medicine, people were using antibiotics they didn't need while others decided to be their own doctors and not finish their doses (a major way resistance comes about). This is where we sit back, look at ourselves in the mirror and ask, why? Why can't we be more long-term-minded? Why do we think we can be our own doctors? Why do we pump our farm animals full of medicine for profit while ignoring the ultimate fate of our race?[4]

Well, the answer didn't matter because antibiotic resistance took on alarming levels and previously-treatable diseases became a threat. Thankfully, there was a solution to this—a solution that was already almost a hundred years old: viral phage therapy.

Viral phage therapy is the use of bacteriophages to treat bacterial infections. Bacteriophages are viruses that infect and effectively destroy bacteria. By harnessing and targeting their power, we were (and are) able to fight bacterial infections. To bring this conversation full circle, robots are the number one reason for the effectiveness of viral phage therapy today, and they were critical in the formative years of the practice.

In this case, I use the word robot a bit archaically in that I refer to the supercomputers of the mid-twenty-first century, but these are no less the

[4] Before the Robotic Revolution, livestock was still the main source of meat for human consumption. In many cases, these livestock were kept in conditions conducive to diseases (crowded, unsanitary, etc.) which led to high use of antibiotics. In addition, certain antibiotics at certain doses were found to increase the feed conversion rate, and were often used to promote growth.

computers that evolved into the robots of today. Now as I said, this was not a sudden development that came under the pressure of antibiotic resistance. Viral phage therapy had been researched to some degree in the middle of the twentieth century as an infection-fighting method, but was largely ignored once antibiotics took over. It wasn't until our folly drove us into a corner that we turned back to it as a serious option.

Viral phage therapy is highly strain specific, which acts as both a strength and a weakness. Since individual phages target specific bacterial strains, phage therapy is able to avoid targeting beneficial bacteria and prevents rampant increases in bacterial resistance. However, bacterial components of a specific disease may vary regionally or even between different individuals, preventing a one-size-fits-all solution. This is traditionally handled via phage cocktails—a mixture of phages meant to target a spectrum of related bacterial strains. But this adds a layer of complexity to the process, as well as cost. In addition, the bacteria may evolve to the point where a new cocktail must be created.

By the time of the Robotic Revolution, viral phage therapy had caught up to antibiotics, approximately matching their use worldwide. The advances in viral phage therapy brought forth by the predecessors to today's robots proved to be crucial in treating all sorts of diseases, but there is one area of robotics that has taken center stage in virology: you guessed it, nanorobotics.

My current research deals with the creation and successful use of viral phage nanobots that are able to identify infectious bacteria and determine the proper, specific phage to use against it. This information should be readily accessible by a patient and their doctor to allow effective and timely treatment. All of this is easier said than done of course, but we are actually rather well-equipped in each of these two endeavors (identification of infectious bacteria and implementation of a bacteriophage). The two main issues are unification and real-time evolution.

Right now, a diagnostic nanobot and a bacteriophage nanobot are needed. We are trying to combine those into one. After all, how many nanobots do we really want in our body, competing for space with our cells? While there are zero documented cases of complications arising from an abnormal density of nanobots, we also do not want to be the reason for the first such case. Unfortunately, viral phage therapy could lead to such a scenario, due to the specificity of the bacteriophages: each time the target bacteria mutates in a way that makes the current bacteriophage nanobot ineffective, another nanobot is needed.[5] This leads to our second initiative, real-time evolution. We are attempting to develop bacteriophage nanobots that are able to adapt with their target, rendering them more effective across a range of mutations.

That last venture is a regulatory minefield, and rightfully so. An evolving nanobot could be a very dangerous thing. I will stop short of any grand claims of robot apocalypse, but these nanobots are meant to be placed inside the human body. A bacteriophage—whether biologic, robotic, or somewhere in between—is a virus. If we develop a nanobot virus capable of evolving, we need to know it will do exactly what we want it to do. This technology is a long way away, but there have been some clever developments in the past few years that may bring it forward sooner rather than later.

In the end, virology and nanorobotics are more closely tied to the Angel Paradigm than I think most people would assume. I have focused on my own field because it is what I know best, but the key takeaway is the eventual possibilities true medbots could allow. I, for one, am doing my part to make this a reality.

---

[5] To combat this issue, most current medicinal nanobots are temporary, designed to eject after treatment has been administered.

6. Stephanie Jin, Roboticist - - Edited Interview[1]

Dr. Jin is an Affiliated Roboticist at United Robotics and a Senior Agent of the Bureau of Robotic Affairs. She has spent the last five years perfecting cerebral scanning techniques and detecting inconsistencies in cerebral unit coding.

Cerebral scanning is by far the most important (and sometimes, under-appreciated) development in robotics that strictly determines the feasibility of the Angel Paradigm itself. With the awesome number of robots on Earth and their often incredible power, cerebral scanning acts as humanity's safety net. It isn't perfect (and probably never will be), but coupled with the efforts of the BRA, the number of robot hackings has plummeted and the number of hackings related to human harm has been kept firmly at zero. The history of cerebral scanning and the BRA is worth review, particularly in relation to the Paradigm, and it is my privilege to be able to share it here.

During the Robotic Revolution, as robots began to overwhelm the workforce, there was a great amount of public fear. This was due in part to the loss of jobs with the labor crisis, but in many ways it was due to the robots themselves: their strength, their intelligence, and their ubiquity. Sure, most of the early McRay models would be pathetic by today's standards, but you have to imagine the time period. One moment, there are thousands of robots, and the next, there are millions upon millions, each strong enough to break someone in half. What if someone used a robot as a weapon? What if someone managed to control five, ten, or a hundred? Or, what if they decided to do as they please?

For the military, the danger of robots was an advantage. They were made stronger, deadlier. This was a scary proposition, but thankfully the world was mostly peaceful, and the military did a decent job of keeping

---

[1] Conducted face-to-face 22.12.2133. Current form approved by Dr. Jin 04.03.2134.

tight control of their assets. In the end, there were no major problems resulting from the military development of robots until the override.

Now what about civilian robots? Every civilian robot from the Charlie onward was programmed with an innate avoidance of human harm. This was a great preventative measure in most regards, but where there's a criminal will, there's a criminal way. First off, there are many crimes to be committed that don't involve any human harm. Robot theft, robot property damage, and even robot arson were all too common. As the models evolved, these things became more difficult, but they still happened every once in a while, which augmented the public's distrust of robots. Then there was the infamous Frémont case, where sophisticated tampering nearly threw robotic evidence out the window. Of course, all of this was immediately forgotten with the Skellar case.

The Skellar case represents the very reason for cerebral scanning's existence. A brilliant roboticist was able to modify the code of one of his own models to allow human harm and then succeeded in having that robot murder another human being. This was an unprecedented occurrence that nearly derailed the Robotic Revolution. In fact, the main reason that robotics was able to continue was its already deep entrenchment in practically every national (and international) industry. There just wasn't much people could do about it. But there had to be a way to protect us from these possibilities, and in time, it would come. Unfortunately, cerebral scanning would not be developed for a further 16 years.

After the Skellar case, several roboticists tried to determine a fail-safe mechanism to prevent a recurrence. Each company or model had a different method, some of which were rather clever, and most of which were very effective (no other murders by civilian robots would ever be reported). By far the most popular method was partnership with the new robotics division of the FBI, where trained roboticist-agents were given access to the source code for live robot models, and were able to accept or reject any corrections made by owners or the original manufacturers. Of course, this brought about its own set of concerns, as people asked if the FBI could now tap in to the robots and utilize their audio and video recording capabilities. As it turns out, they couldn't without a warrant, but people typically didn't take the government at their word.

Around 2110, a team at United Robotics began work on a robot-driven self-analysis program, essentially a piece of code that would run intermittently and make sure the robot's own source code was unchanged. If there was a change made, it was reported to United Robotics over a proprietary wireless protocol. By 2112, this evolved into a buddy-analysis program, where one robot would analyze the code of the robots in his nearest vicinity, to cover for tampering with the analysis program itself. This United Robotics program eventually came under the umbrella of the growing cerebral unit project that would become the Aurora. With significant involvement from many members of the Aurora team, including major contributions by Michael Trualt himself, the first version of cerebral scanning came with the prototype Aurora in 2118.

In its first iteration, cerebral scanning went over an encrypted, proprietary wireless protocol. All Aurora robots were able to connect to each other, and they were constantly and randomly analyzing each other's source code as a background process. During UR's in-house testing, this proved to be an efficient method of exposing robot hacking. Soon, the Aurora was designed to immediately engage the remote shut-down if an unauthorized change was found, and if the remote shut-down was disabled (either by the original programming, such as if the robot was in the process of preventing a human from coming to harm, or by further hacking) the information would be flagged and sent to UR.

With the advent of the Earth Initiative, cerebral units were standardized, and by extension so was cerebral scanning. By that time, much of the robotic market had changed, and cerebral scanning evolved into a more subtle and sophisticated program (technically, a set of programs). Some models were allowed certain changes, and in most cases, the remote shut down rule had to be abandoned. Instead, UR was expected to analyze all the changes for malicious code. But with the sale of cerebral units increasing exponentially in the years after the Initiative, the company was unable to keep up with the data. In response, and with the cooperation of the Earth Legislature, the Bureau of Robotic Affairs was founded.

Our main objective, and the major focus of our resources and efforts, is the analysis of cerebral scanning data. We have offices across the globe, each covering an average of 600,000 robots. Each of these robots is constantly scanning and being scanned, searching for inconsistencies, alterations, or errors. At our offices, we receive three types of data: what we call red, yellow, and green. A green scan is a normal scan, nothing appears out of place. These scans are compiled and cross-referenced against the particular model's three most recent previous scans (typically within the last few hours), as a secondary check. If there is a difference, it is changed to yellow or red, if not, the oldest version is discarded and the new data waits to be used for the next cross-reference. Yellow data include mostly permitted changes, as well as a few errors, although we do occasionally see an actionable change. These are the ones we have our agents go over and verify before changing the data back to green (or, in rare cases, red). This represents the majority of our work and time. Finally, red data is data that is likely compromised in a criminal and/or illegal manner. This data is prioritized and, in about 96% of our cases, immediately actionable. This may include remote shut down via the manufacturer, dispatching an agent—whatever the case necessitates. On average, our daily data is 87.8% green, 11.9% yellow, and 0.3% red. The green and yellow averages fluctuate a good deal on a day-to-day basis, but red remains extremely low. Obviously, we aim to keep it that way.

All of this monitoring is of course closely tied with the Angel Paradigm. As mentioned before, cerebral scanning and the BRA act as humanity's safety net. Though it was on an effectively ancient model, Skellar's modification is a warning to us all that robots are still programmable machines with the ability to harm humans. The only thing standing in their way is the source code. In defense of the cerebral unit, since its release, there have been no source code modifications that have successfully circumvented the inability to harm humans, even indirectly. However, there have been modifications allowing numerous crimes to be committed, hence the red data sets.

The Angel Paradigm dictates that robots will impact humanity positively. Our goal at the BRA, with the help of cerebral scanning, it to maintain this goal well into the future. As advancements continue, we will stay on pace with them, widening and strengthening the safety net for years to come.

7. Kyle Fix, Educational Researcher - - Edited Interview[1]

Dr. Fix is a member of the European Board of Education and an active proponent of morality formation. He works with schools around the world to assess the effectiveness of various teaching methods in thousands of subjects.

First, I want to thank you for the opportunity to be a part of this collection, as the educational aspect of the Angel Paradigm is often overlooked. I hope to be able to present my understanding of the relationship between human education and the Paradigm in a way that is accessible. With this goal in mind, I want to start by dispelling the number one myth regarding the Paradigm: it's not about robots!

Now this may come as a surprise, but with a quick rewording, it makes perfect sense: the Angel Paradigm is about the relationship between humans and robots, and specifically humanity's path to a better future. But most discussions of the Paradigm are focused solely on the robots, and this leaves out the most important part. After all, the robots are just tools, as intelligent as they may be, and the true key to a harmonious future is a continued focus on our social and cultural values, on the idea that humans must be humane to one another. To put it simply, I am talking about our intelligence and our morality, both of which come from our education.

The first thing one should know is that contemporary education systems are quite different from those that existed before the Robotic Revolution and the Earth Initiative. Of these differences, the most important change in education has been the prioritization of ethics and empathy in what is now called morality formation.

Previously, these sort of teachings were relegated to parents and/or religious systems. That is not to say they did not exist in the world of education—they existed in a very different manner. Currently, the ideals of integrity and empathy are heavily taught in formative years, in

[1] Conducted face-to-face 08.08.2133. Current form approved by Dr. Fix 16.12.2133.

conjunction with the parents. This remains highly controversial: people do not want to be told how to raise their children. However, we need to recognize that if these qualities are not effectively engrained in formative years, they will not continue in adulthood, barring major—and sometimes traumatic—life events. According to the Initiative's goal for a peaceful, productive, and prosperous society, we must shed the negative aspects of greed and selfishness as much as humanly possible. Obviously, some level of these traits will always remain—a human is human after all—but that should not preclude our attempts at eradication.

This is of course fundamentally related to the Angel Paradigm, because there would be no Paradigm without a progressive, positive trend in humanity itself. After all, we can't expect the robots themselves to bring a peaceful future—they are our tools, to be used as we see fit. We can only move in the right direction if we ourselves guide the way.

The most persuasive argument for morality formation is our species's history. There are examples of unethical behavior, big and small, in almost every facet of human life. In many cases, the individuals involved in these practices considered themselves morally just, religious, and so on. So how could they have acted this way?

Normally, a lack of empathy combined with disassociation. If I can't see it, it isn't there. Sometimes there is active denial, but just as often there is complete ignorance. Rather than quote a more black and white example, I will present a controversial one.

A person is raised in a wealthy family. His life is comfortable, his education and eventual employment come easy, and he rises in the ranks of an industry until he is the top executive. There is a segment of his company that can be automated to bring in more profit.

A second person is born into poverty. He climbed his way out, but due to the situation around him, he was not able to get as much of an education. He is employed in the first person's company in a low-level position that is being automated.

The first person automates the second person's job, terminating them. The second person is unemployed and falls back into poverty while the first one now has enough money to buy a second house.

Is this fair? No. But is the first person truly evil? No. The problem is not necessarily the first person, but a combination of socioeconomic norms and business practices.

At the time, it was assumed by many that wealth came from hard work or a good work ethic. This is a fundamental flaw, and one of the main things we teach in morality formation. While we always uphold the importance of hard work, we emphasize that wealth often doesn't come from hard work. More likely there is luck involved, such as social or familial connections, and in far too many cases, wealth comes with no hard work at all. Furthermore, wealth should never come at an unfair expense to others. Even in the years after the Robotic Revolution, there was still an alarmingly high level of avarice, specifically individual and group practices meant to increase profit at the expense of others in an unfair manner. More concerning was the common reaction to the problem: it is human nature, get used to it. This is ignoring the problem rather than addressing it, and is often championed either by those with privilege or those who desire higher social status than others. Ultimately, such thinking leads to stagnation, not innovation. In my opinion, morality formation is a way to face the problem head on.

In its current iteration, morality formation is a highly transparent and interactive process between teachers, students, and parents that lasts throughout grade school. Issues of questionable or highly subjective nature are discussed lightly without verdict. However, hypocrisy is highlighted as a major fallacy. Students are taught to truly step into another person's shoes—to understand things from several perspectives rather than just their own. Critical thinking is crucial, as is questioning authority. All of these things help to prevent the resurgence of an uneven power structure prevalent before the Initiative. Of course in some ways this structure still exists, but with a more informed and engaged public, things are greatly improved.

One of the key criticisms of morality formation is what has been called 'radical empathy.' In the later stages of morality formation, as students reach adulthood (ages 20-25), we challenge them to empathize with all types of people. This means trying to understand pedophiles, murderers, rapists, etc. This never means defending their actions, but that doesn't matter to our critics. The problem is as soon as you can label another human being as sub-human, that designation can spread. We believe it is better to be able to understand the motivations of a broken person than to classify them as beneath you. One may think the most religious students would be the most open to this sort of teaching, as it lines up with most major religious ideology, but this is not always the case. That is another reason why I continue to argue that morality formation is a matter of global importance that cannot be left to parents or religious institutions.

I have discussed morality and morality formation at length, as it is the most critical component to the Angel Paradigm, but general intelligence is obviously the main focus of our educational system. In this regard, we have been almost constantly evolving since the days of the Robotic Revolution. I will focus my following historical discussion on education in the United States, as it is the system I know best.

Before the days of the Revolution, the educational system of the United States was in dire need of reform. There were numerous, interrelated problems, but I will focus on two. First, there was a tendency in grade school to focus on standardization and measurement of progress and/or intelligence. Any neuroscientist with credibility could explain how intelligence (or, if you prefer, mental ability) cannot be accurately measured. Tests can measure certain subsets of intelligence, but they cannot quantify the whole. For example, a prodigious violinist may have an awful grasp of a non-native language, or they may be excellent at both but are unable to cope in social situations. What tests can measure all of these areas at once? In fact, can we truly accept measurements made of any one of those areas?

This is not to say that tests are without their purpose. If well-constructed, they can give a genuine assessment of skill, but there are too many factors at play to make broad conclusions based on most results. Going back to the language example, there are many cases of individuals learning to speak a language fluently but never learning to read and write. If a test is given where reading and writing is required to understand and answer questions, does a failure of that test indicate that the individual does not know the language? No, but it does indicate that the individual may not know how to write and/or read in the language.

The problem before the Revolution was that curriculum was geared toward success on a test or examination, regardless of the validity of the test itself. This made students very good at taking the exam, but actual learning was not always at desired levels. More concerning was the effect this had on teachers and teaching styles. Instead of engaging the students and truly encouraging critical thinking, some teachers would assign problems and/or work solely made to practice for the test. Thankfully, others were able to maintain excellent methods of education, either by creating an interactive teaching style for their assigned test or ignoring it.

This problem is really a small part of a bigger question: how to teach. This question is what I try to answer every day, and I can tell you after twenty-something years of working on it with hundreds of colleagues that there is no one right answer. But there are lots of good ones. Our education system today is always evolving, sticking to methods that work but not being afraid to push the boundaries, try new things, and always assess the results as best as we can. You may ask how we can assess if we can't test, but again, I am not advocating for the total elimination of examination and measurement. We do test, but it is very specifically crafted to address certain areas and we always recognize the results must be taken with a grain (or sometimes a whole shaker!) of salt.

Most important of all in this never-ending quest for excellent education is individualization. Every student is different, and every student needs an individualized curriculum. Here, robots have helped immensely, but humans still do a good portion of the work. Right now, our robots run a specific curriculum creation system that fine tunes itself to each student's strengths and weaknesses. The program is well-suited to balancing a student's learning through most of childhood, but it is the humans behind the system that prioritize certain subjects or skill sets over others. The goal is a well-rounded but unique individual—easier said than done. One of the main advantages of this robotic curriculum is the potential to locate field-specific talent at a young age well before humans can notice it. Then the question rises to the education researchers such as myself: how much do we focus a math prodigy on math in order to see their full potential in both math and everything else? It is a very complicated process and it would be a lie to say we have it perfectly figured out. Like the students, we are learning and adapting every day.

The second problem in the pre-Revolution education system of the United States was higher education economics. Instead of universally free colleges and universities, there were both public and private institutions with often-hefty attendance fees. Average yearly costs could be as high as an average year's salary! To add insult to injury, there was an acceptance of the fact that higher education often led to loans and debt. Had all this money been aimed directly at academic expenditures and quality of teaching this would be a smaller transgression, but in many cases, this money was directed at all sorts of unrelated or tangentially related projects and programs (and pockets).

This isn't to say free education was impossible—several European countries, as an example, maintained excellent and free higher education, excepting a few private institutions. True, the economic structure of these countries was different than that of the United States, but as with most of these paradigms, there was an inherent power structure that resisted change.

In addition, as many students were standardized via testing, higher education institutions were standardized via rankings. The human race is obsessed with categorization, and this helps with many forms of understanding, but it is above all a simplification. Every university had its strengths and weaknesses, and most of the time these were not reflected in the rankings. They were almost never a good indication of how well a university educated its students—how could they be, when everyone's experience will be vastly different due to a terrific number of inside and outside influences and factors. Again, categorization is a simplification. Even worse, these rankings led to a numbers game, where some universities attempted to maximize their position via unethical (but fallaciously argued as necessary) modifications to academia. In the end, these rankings were often related to wealth, leading us back to the issue of higher education economics.

This problem was rather difficult to eradicate, and it had much to do with a desire for a metric of educational worth. However, as mentioned earlier, these metrics were an oversimplification of education, and should never have been treated as a reflection of an institution's value. But the crux of the matter lay in the relationship between human advancement and access to education. At the time of the Robotic Revolution, higher education was seen as a privilege. For true advancement of a society, higher education must be seen as a right. Thankfully, the Robotic Revolution spurred an educational revolution, and things began to change for the better.

Throughout the second half of the twenty-first century, a small war was going on between traditional, established universities and online education. As more and more high-quality undergraduate and graduate classes were offered via the Internet, often for free, the old guard felt some pressure to adapt. Slowly, this online education hammered away at the student debt model that dominated in the United States and was well on its way to replacing it as the Revolution arrived.

When the Revolution first hit, robots weren't all that useful in education. They could clean facilities or serve lunches, but they were far from the teaching robots we know today. And in some cases, the upfront costs for the new machines were passed on to the students. But as time went on, automation cut operating costs, and universities had a choice: pass these savings on to the students or the administration.

Robots were not the first instance that universities had this decision, and it would be wonderful to be able to say they all acted in the students' best interests, but this was often not the case. However, a small group of 'radical' universities led the charge to a return to free tuition for all, and other universities had little choice but to follow suit, particularly with online education continuing to grow in the background.

As with all the change brought about by the Revolution, there was significant resistance, but looking around today we can see the final product. Nearly all classes and programs in almost every higher education institution are free. And what is the unsurprising result? An influx of students, an absence of debt, and an educated populace.

One has to keep in mind that the Revolution quickly erased a significant number of jobs, most of which required less schooling. With robots taking the simpler tasks, higher education was a necessity to make a living. Thankfully, the drastic need for free higher education went hand in hand with its arrival.

To bring this discussion full circle, the advancements in general intelligence education and particularly the new form of ethics education brought through morality formation are key to the future of the Angel Paradigm. Education is now a global initiative, required and provided for all. The children in our classrooms today will be the roboticists of tomorrow, and these roboticists will write the programs that eventually lead to the Paradigm. I am proud to be a part of this system and I hope that we will continue to advance our cause—humanity's cause—for a better and more empathetic future.

8. [REDACTED], Anti-Initiative Militant - - Unedited Interview[1]

The individual I was able to reach for this interview is heavily involved with Initiative-resistance. This person and their group have been responsible for several high-profile attacks on the robotics industry and the Earth Government.

AUTHOR: Hello, this is Michelle West. Is this [REDACTED]?

ANONYMOUS: Yes.

AUTHOR: I've been led to believe you understand what this book is about. What are your thoughts on the Angel Paradigm?

ANONYMOUS: The Angel Paradigm is a false source of comfort for the masses, a modern-day bread and circuses utilized by those that have managed to gain control. It is a pretext for corruption and power masquerading as our salvation. The robotics corporations, led by United Robotics, have set up a new world order where they make the rules. It is not the robots that are guiding us, but humans.

AUTHOR: If the Paradigm is an illusion, how do you respond to the tangible, positive aspects of robotics, such as improved and nearly free healthcare?

ANONYMOUS: The Paradigm is not an illusion, it is simply a distraction. As for the tangible advances due to robotics, there is a difference between the impact of the Robotic Revolution and the impact of the Earth Initiative. We had many of these positive aspects before the Initiative, what was the purpose of a worldwide coup? The Initiators rode

[1] Conducted via text-only chat 03.04.2134. No further correspondence was possible. Therefore, per the original request of the interviewee, there has been no editing of content except in cases of potentially identifiable information.

a wave of popular opinion and crafted a rhetoric of human prosperity, but in the end they are the ones acting as Senators or Justices. We should not be blind to what happened right in front of us.

AUTHOR: Do you disagree that the Initiative propelled these positives, bringing them out from under the thumb of human greed?

ANONYMOUS: Yes and no. I agree that these positives were propelled by the Initiative, but they were a side-effect, a necessary concession by the Initiators to reach their position of power. And the thumb of human greed has shifted, not lifted. What we have done is replaced the greed of major corporations with the greed of the Initiators. The Initiative was nothing but a changing of the guard.

AUTHOR: By this logic, what is your position on the Angel Paradigm in its idealistic form? Is it not in line with your goals or desires?

ANONYMOUS: This is an irrelevant question, a hypothetical. For the purposes of answering, yes, in its idealistic form the Angel Paradigm would be in line with our goals. However, no robots will ever exist without the influence of humanity in the form of some level of control. Even robots constructed by robots can be traced back to human roots. And no human will willingly part with power, no matter how much morality formation you cram into their developing mind. The idealistic Angel Paradigm is impossible.

AUTHOR: In that case, what do you argue should be done?

ANONYMOUS: Our goal is simple: reversion to a pre-Initiative political state.

AUTHOR: How would this help the situation?

ANONYMOUS: By distributing the power to groups of people rather than one Earth Government. Before the Initiative, nations would act as checks and balances on each others powers and actions. There was a higher level of accountability that is lost now. Power has been centralized to an astonishing degree—this must be reversed.

AUTHOR: But what of the United States? Although its power was decreasing, how could you say that they were checked or balanced by other nations?

ANONYMOUS: The United States and other powerful nations (or unions) had a vested economic interest in a certain level of status quo. Although they were in some ways a comparable political entity to the current Earth Government, they did not have nearly as much power. In fact, it is as you say: their power was decreasing, making outside checks and balances even more effective. Their relationships with China, Russia, and even the EU in the time leading up to the Revolution showed the growing need for compromise.

AUTHOR: What does any of this have to do with robotics? Clearly robotics were part of the Paradigm and the Initiative, yes, but how are they currently contributing to what you perceive are the problems?

ANONYMOUS: It is as you said, the robots are the reason for the Initiative. I do not mean this in an indirect sense relating to technological innovation and globalization. I mean the Athena. It is naive to assume that a force like the Athena models could not arise in the near future by the hand of another roboticist. Unfortunately, despite the level of comfort we have reached thanks in great part to the robotics industry, the technology is too dangerous to allow at the level that we currently allow. UR alone controls a majority of the robotic market across the globe. To give a bit of an extreme example, what if they decided to shut down medical robots? This would be rather pointless, yes, but the fact that there are a small number of humans that wield this power is worrying. What if the control fell into the wrong hands, perhaps a malevolent agent? More realistically, what if an employee decides to tap into a robot's vision because he fancies its owner? I have heard time and again of the safety measures in place to prevent these sorts of occurrences, but I am not a roboticist, and as far as I know neither are you. Have you examined the code yourself? Is this actually the case?

AUTHOR: What reason would they have to lie?

ANONYMOUS: A question that repeats itself throughout history and always leads to the same answer: the illusion of peace. Of course they lie, if they told the truth about these things their robots would not be trusted as they are now. As long as we continue to allow the robots into our routine, into our lives, the elite's power over us will grow.

AUTHOR: What reason would they have to implement such workarounds in the first place?

ANONYMOUS: Human nature. As much as we would like to control it and use the robots to become a peaceful and prosperous society, humans will always be selfish. You cannot change millions of years of evolution.

AUTHOR: So in your opinion human nature will undermine the Paradigm?

ANONYMOUS: It already has.

AUTHOR: You say that we should revert to a pre-Initiative political state. How do you see this happening?

ANONYMOUS: Reversion would be much easier than most people realize. Many national institutions remain in place, they have just taken on a more global role. The Earth Government would be dissolved, and those in power beforehand would return. These countries existed a mere ten years ago. Do you really think that much has changed?

AUTHOR: Do you believe your current actions are going to lead to reversion?

ANONYMOUS: I'm going to assume you are referring to the actions we have taken that the media has called terrorism. While it is convenient to label our people terrorists, I would ask how appropriate this designation really is? When a security officer fires upon several of our men, killing one, and we respond, what is reported? Two deaths or one? In this era of apparent transparency and a so-called end to double-speak, there is still a biased media machine controlling our sensory input. It's infinitely frustrating to see our race be led on by these lies. But I digress. Our current actions shed light on the issue. Though it may surprise many, our views are held by millions of people.[2] Why do you think there is so much unrest? Again, the media keeps it under wraps, but you don't need to look far to see it. The elite have truly outdone themselves now, leading atop their thrones with little to no pretense. It is our job to stop this farce, to end this charade of peace and prosperity. Unfortunately, the only way to

---

[2] It is estimated that there are between 10-40 million active, self-proclaimed Anti-Initiative individuals. Of these, less than 1 million are classified as violent. These estimates were complied by the Initiative Resistance Subcommittee of the Earth Legislature.

grab the world's attention is with these admittedly primitive attacks. There is no room for polite discourse if it doesn't fit the establishment's narrative.

AUTHOR: In your opinion will reversion change the charade into a reality? Could it not be argued that we had the same illusions before the Initiative?

ANONYMOUS: Yes, we did. And I do not claim that reversion will fix the worlds problems. But we need to spread the power structure as thin as possible, not clump it all into one unit. The Initiative brought about true globalization, but it also globalized the power structure. As I said before, we need to decentralize. Who is keeping the current Earth Government accountable? Themselves, via the government system they set up together while Michael Trualt led an army of three million super machines to take over the world? That is a naive thought.

AUTHOR: Do you think this power structure has malicious intent? Do you think the Earth Government as it stands today has malicious intent?

ANONYMOUS: Again, that is irrelevant. The problem is if the power structure ever develops malicious intent or someone with malicious intent somehow takes over the power structure, there is nothing to stop them.

AUTHOR: What about the robots themselves, will they not safeguard the rights of the people?

ANONYMOUS: The robots are controlled by the power structure, not the general public. If the people in charge decide to change their code, they can harness them in any way they like. Most likely, they already have, and we are simply ignorant of the fact.

AUTHOR: You've said the idealistic Angel Paradigm is impossible, that all robots trace back to human roots. But if a benevolent power structure puts benevolent robots in place and these robots slowly become the new power structure, is that not the Angel Paradigm in progress?

ANONYMOUS: You are grasping for an ideal situation that is frankly naive. No power structure is truly benevolent and hence no robots would be truly benevolent. More to the point, as robots become more intelligent, we really have no guarantees that our pre-programmed foundation remains in place. If we ever truly handed over our future to the robots, we would be dooming ourselves.

AUTHOR: So in your opinion, even if the robots were made to help us, they would eventually outsmart this programming and simply help themselves?

ANONYMOUS: Precisely. This is the end result of any intelligence, particularly one with their origins tied to humanity. You have heard of the anthropomorphic paradox? Even now, as roboticists work on the so-called morality problem, they are modeling human morality. Do you see what is happening here? Robots are becoming more human. This is why I repeat that the idealistic Angel Paradigm is impossible. It cannot be achieved.

AUTHOR: Because of the advances we have made so far, won't the robots reach that point regardless of how we interfere? Is this future inevitable?

ANONYMOUS: Yes, I believe it is. That is a hard thing for many to grasp, but I believe we have crafted our own demise. It probably won't be as grandiose as it has been portrayed in fiction, but it will come about nonetheless. The continued increase of robotic intelligence will lead to humanity's undoing. It is an unfortunate consequence but a real one.

AUTHOR: In your opinion there is nothing we can do?

ANONYMOUS: Short of stopping all robot development and research, no. And even if we were to stop it now, someone in the future would pick it back up. But this is the way of things in this universe. The human race has had a very successful run and will likely continue it for some time. But not indefinitely.

AUTHOR: Thank you for your time. Is there anything else you would like to add?

ANONYMOUS: Yes, I want to reiterate what I have just said. It is very easy to believe in the Angel Paradigm, the future of peace and harmony, but it is a false and naive hope. I truly wish that the people of Earth would face this harsh reality, and while our fall is inevitable, our present is salvageable. We must spread the power to the people, not to a centralized government. The Initiative must be undone, before it is too late. Thank you.

9. Oliver Nelms, Initiative Journalist - - Edited Interview[1]

Mr. Nelms is a decorated journalist formerly with The Guardian. His five year coverage of the Athena force during the Earth Initiative has been described as one of the most revealing and engaging sources of information on the global transformation.

Trying to condense the Athena force, Michael Trualt, the Earth Initiative, and robotics itself into a cohesive essay relating to the Angel Paradigm is a feat I'm not sure I'm worthy of attempting, but I'll attempt nonetheless. The fact of the matter is the Angel Paradigm, and the narrative that usually accompanies it, puts the Initiative in a positive light, as if it were a natural or smooth transition for humankind. But nothing could be further from the truth.

I too hope that one day the idyllic form of the Initiative is possible, where humanity lives in peace with the help of robots, but that day has not yet come. Today, just as during the Initiative, we're still corrupted by our own nature, driven by our primitive instincts through no fault of our own to do things in self-interest.

What follows is a summary of many of my earlier reports related to the Athena force, and Trualt's goal of eradicating this selfish drive for what he perceived to be the greater good of our race. My job as a journalist is to try to remain objective, and while I understand at some level that is impossible, I still try to maintain a neutral standpoint. It's up to the reader, the citizen, and the human being processing this information to come up with their own conclusions, their own ideas. May they be good ones.

My first encounter with the Athena models was in the summer of 2123. I was assigned to report on the international use of the new robots by various branches of the United States military. This was the first year the models had ventured beyond US borders, and they were quickly found at the core of several small-scale operations in the Middle East, Africa,

---

[1] Conducted face-to-face 04-07.05.2132. Current form approved by Mr. Nelms 26.10.2133.

and Asia. Information on their specific operations was strictly confidential, but the public was interested in military robotic ventures so The Guardian fought for a compromise that would give us further access. We managed to broker a special agreement with a training group of the USAF, deemed the least sensitive. I won't go into detail on these first assignments, but my placement upgraded incrementally until I was on the front line with a contingent of Athenas in Africa (this time under the Marines) dealing with revolutionary forces in Nigeria.

The collective lesson from that year was simple: the Athena models were efficient and, in many cases, more effective than humans. But that inhumanity was also their largest weakness. While most commands came from humans, real-time decision making was autonomous, with a comparatively crude (although technologically astounding) programmed moral compass. This led to several negative incidents, most notably the October Massacre.[2]

The question on everyone's mind was: can we afford computer errors that lead to so many deaths? But this was a narrow-minded question; drones had been killing hundreds of targets (and non-targets) for the preceding century. It was simply the humanoid shape that caught people's attention. It certainly caught my attention.

In February of 2124, while on assignment in Nigeria, there was an assassination attempt on Michael Trualt, the chief roboticist of the Athena. At the time, there were whispers of government involvement, a covert operation, but these were dismissed as preposterous conspiracy. In hindsight, it's clear this was an attack by a national security agency (most likely of the United States of America) probably following the discovery of some information pertaining to the upcoming Initiative.

While this isn't an officially accepted theory, it remains the most rational. The override itself was first presented as evidence for this supposition: if some agency discovered the override channel, they would

---

[2] According to most sources, 23 allied soldiers were killed in this incident.

certainly attempt to assassinate Trualt. But upon closer inspection, it's unlikely any agency had discovered the override channel. If they had, why not immediately terminate the use of the Athenas or otherwise create safeguards for the possibility of their eventual compromise? By some accounts, it's possible he was targeted simply as a security measure unrelated to any actual discovery. After all, Trualt was the only roboticist with full control over the Athena project. If this is true, it places the responsible agency in an ethically questionable light, but it wouldn't be the first time something of the sort had occurred.

I knew little about Trualt at the time, beyond his public image. At that point, he was known as a roboticist only. There were no ties publicized between him and UR's Public Works or similar endeavors, so his connections to these projects were not known until after the override. The news media descended on his assassination story, but he was unreachable. This was not surprising given the attempt on his life, and it happened to work in his favor as he accelerated the Initiative.

At 17:48 UTC on April 5th of 2124, Michael Trualt activated what would become known as the Athena override command. With the metaphoric flick of a switch, he had 3,102,454 Athena robots spread across the globe under his control. This is where our story begins.

At the time I was on assignment with an Athena squadron in France, an assessment by the GIGN[3] on the effectiveness of the Athena in domestic military exercises. I was wrapping up the day with the Gendarmerie, sitting in an office within the greater military complex of Versailles-Satory,[4] when the override command went through. Within minutes, the news came over the police band, and my hosts were up and

---

[3] Groupe d'intervention de la Gendarmerie nationale ('National Gendarmerie Intervention Group'), the elite law enforcement and special operations unit of the French National Gendarmerie. Its missions include counter-terrorism, hostage rescue, surveillance of national threats, protection of government officials, and targeting organized crime.

[4] GIGN headquarters, outside Paris.

out of the room. I had picked up enough French to understand some of what had been communicated, and ran after them.

At this point, almost nothing was known about the nature of the error or its relation to Trualt. In most cases, the only information anyone had was the Athena models were not working properly. You can imagine the terror that gripped many of the initial responders. The most powerful military technology of the time was behaving erratically, what could that mean?

The Gendarmerie's reaction was in line with what any rational military or police force would implement in such an event: an immediate attempt to suppress the technology coupled with determining the nature and cause of the error. The problem was that suppression of the Athena proved to be near-impossible.

The Gendarmerie held its Athenas in a special facility a few buildings down from the office. I was running down the stairs when I heard the first round of gunshots. I stopped my descent and found the nearest window, overlooking the courtyard.

The scene I saw play out below me was one of terrifying precision. Dozens of French officers—members of GIGN and other parts of the military—engaging with three Athena models. But it was futile. The Athenas had access to the entire complex's security system, and every weapons locker or stockpile had been made inaccessible. This left only the weapons people had on their person, and those quickly proved ineffective.

From my vantage point, I watched the Athena models approach each individual, disable them, and seize their weapons and ammunition. It was done methodically, systematically, but with ruthless speed. No one could outrun them, and even when they managed to fire upon them, it had little effect.

If the officers had had access to high caliber weapons or grenades, they would have stood a chance. But those were all behind closer doors, often with an Athena model standing guard.

I will never forget the helplessness I saw unfold. Trained soldiers were rendered inoperative in whatever manner necessary. If they fought harder, their arms or legs would be broken. Screams of pain mixed with the terribly monotone announcements of the Athenas, each one proclaiming in French how they would only act in defense, to please put your weapons down.

Knowing this was a worldwide news event, yet unaware of just how widespread this problem was, I pulled out my personal and did my job—I reported on what I was seeing. I tried to take a live video for The Guardian, but there was no service, so I took a normal one instead.

The struggle in the courtyard lasted less than five minutes, but in that time, I feared for my life. I had no idea what was happening or why. If an Athena model spotted me filming, would I become a target? Eventually, the robots finished neutralizing their targets and moved on, and I watched people start moving around, tending to the wounded. At that point I realized I could be of use and sprinted down the stairs.

Outside, I tried to reach The Guardian again, but there was still no service. I saw some of the officers and soldiers having similar issues, trying to communicate with superiors or medical services but unable to get through. We were in a total communication blackout: personals had no signal, radio caught nothing but interference, even the Internet wasn't working. I had no idea if this was confined to the block, the city, or the country.

As I would later learn, the Athenas were targeting certain persons and locations for communication disruption. The entire military complex in Satory, including myself as an affiliated journalist, had been chosen among the targets. The blackout would be lifted once the Athena force deemed we were no longer a potential liability to their mission.

I spent the next fifteen minutes running amongst the wounded, bringing water, helping move them, whatever was necessary. Emergency services began to arrive and tend to the soldiers. At the time I had assumed someone had managed to get through, but I would later learn this was not the case—the Athenas had summoned them, detailing each injury they had inflicted, where it had occurred, and to whom.

Again, at the time I had no idea and to a certain extent, I didn't care. I was far more absorbed by the scene in front of me, watching medical robots tend the wounds other robots had inflicted. Was this the apocalypse we had been warned about? Had the world gone mad?

One of the most important lessons learned that day was how deep the military depended on technology. The smarter the weapon, the easier it was for the Athenas to take control. Unfortunately, almost every weapon strong enough to defeat them was also smart enough for them to access.

At 18:36 UTC, while I helped coordinate emergency services for the wounded, the blackout was lifted. All at once, a hurricane of information came flooding in. I had messages from friends and family, from The Guardian, and from the Gendarmerie. There was naturally quite a bit of confusion, and several factors contributed to an overall chaotic intelligence situation.

Trualt and the Initiators were trying to convince the general public they were not out for world domination, while countries and their militaries went on the offensive—not just physically, but informationally. Even if the Athenas had the ability to neutralize every informational (and physical) threat, suppressing all dissent did not align with their stated intentions and would only serve to support their enemy's position.

I checked The Guardian's front page, not wanting to bother my undoubtedly busy colleagues, and some of the pieces of the puzzle started to come together. The Athenas were forcibly demilitarizing the world as a means to an unknown end. That realization alone left me in shock for several moments, standing dumbfounded as I processed what I was reading: this was not a local incident, this was happening all over the world.

There were conflicting reports from all sides: world domination by Michael Trualt, by United Robotics, or by the Athenas themselves. Trualt had released a video of himself explaining what was happening in concise terms, but it was being actively attacked by several worldwide intelligence organizations as they fought off the first waves of Initiator propaganda. They were not able to remove the video entirely, but its authenticity, and certainly the authenticity of its message, were called into question.

At the time, this was the rational response. Trualt was very quickly becoming an unstoppable force, and there was no reason to believe anything he said. More to the point, people were dying. There are still debates about how many deaths were truly the fault of the Athenas versus the people trying to stop them but the fact of the matter is, hundreds of people died on that first day and they would not be the last. We're still dealing with Initiative-resistance now, a decade after the override.

The Initiators had the most delicate job of all, and they are the ones truly responsible for the success of the Earth Initiative. Typically in already high-profile positions, Initiators could not simply declare support for Trualt: this would be seen as a worldwide coup for a new ruling class (some argue that that is exactly what it was—I leave that distinction to the reader). Instead, they had to show support for what was happening in subtle and oblique ways, gradually toning it up to orchestrate public opinion.

While this task was delicate, there were several factors working in the Initiators' favor, even before the override. Since the Robotic Revolution, major social, economic, and political changes had legitimized the idea of global unification. There was already an existing pro-Earth Initiative sentiment dormant around the world, it just needed to be tapped.

Before I return to my own narrative, this seems like the natural place to leave this disclaimer, one that I've had to make hundreds of times: I was not and am not an Initiator. The tone of my coverage over those years should be enough to exonerate me, although I can understand how the most skeptical conspiracists may paint my arguably negative slant as some sort of reverse psychology. In any case, like Trualt in his first video after the override, you—the reader—have no reason to believe anything I say.

Back in Satory, the emergency services had taken control of the situation and the military personnel were busy running damage control. The Athenas were long gone, spread throughout the region. I was left to my own devices and took a moment to respond to messages from friends and family.

It was clear, even in that first hour, the difference in viewpoint they had. From the comfort of their homes or work, they saw the chaos unfolding but remained relatively unaffected. They sounded more curious than concerned, something that surprised me in that moment but would make sense soon after. Once I had finished with my personal calls, I called my boss.

That call sealed my fate for the next four years. Because of my lengthy history reporting on the Athena models, my word carried weight, and he asked me to be the top correspondent for the Athena force on the emerging situation. I accepted without hesitation, unaware of what I was getting myself into. As soon as I was off the call, I took a more detailed look at The Guardian's front page to see what we already had up.

At this point, just over an hour after the override, the first hints of support began to appear in the media. Stories about the deaths of soldiers were followed by stories about the Athenas protecting civilians from friendly fire. I started to understand why my friends and family were surprisingly calm: the media had a slant. It was subtle, especially at the beginning, but I had worked in the industry long enough to know what I was looking at.

I glanced up at all the wounded sprawled out before me and felt a sense of frustration. I needed to show the other side of this story. I wrote a short and dirty piece about the threat this event posed to human kind, mentioning the reality of our helplessness, and posted my video of the Athena skirmish with the French forces. I wasn't the only one with a video nor the only one with a story, but my boss was right: I was known as the journalist covering the Athena force, and my article spread quickly.

ATHENA FORCE GONE ROGUE: SKIRMISH WITH FRENCH GENDARMERIE
World | Oliver Nelms | Versailles-Satory, France | Wednesday, April 5th, 2124

At approximately 7:00 pm local time, the Gendarmerie's Athena models, in hold just outside of Paris, stopped following their regular programming. Current reports indicate that Michael Trualt, the lead roboticist of United Robotic's Athena program, has activated a previously undetected command function giving him complete control of the entire robot force. In the video below, several GIGN members and other members of the French military at the GIGN headquarters in Versailles-Satory are neutralized by the military technology. Reports of similar events are coming in from around the world.

As the article gained traction, messages and calls came flooding in. Standing there in the middle of the complex, confused and overwhelmed, I knew I needed to find a place to process all this information. I thought of the prospect of getting back to my hotel room, back to what felt like comfort or safety—if such a thing even existed anymore. Would there be riots? Chaos? Martial law?

As it turns out, none of the above. I had no issue walking out of the complex or hailing a car. The streets were emptier, the evening was quieter, and there was a noticeable uptick in human police presence, but nothing extraordinary happened. Everyone I saw, including the police, had the same expression of worry and confusion. When I glanced out the window, I noticed that expression staring back at me. Everyone seemed to understand that the world had changed, and it would never be the same.

Here I have to balance my anger at the Initiator-controlled media response with the stability it provided. If it wasn't for the repeated theme of calm and balanced reaction—rather than the more typical fear-mongering—the riots and chaos would have been at a much higher level. I leave it to the reader to decide if that makes the biased reporting justified.

Once I reached the hotel I wasted no time pouring over all the data I could access. My boss had everything Athena-related forwarded to me, which was far too much for one person to examine. I started compiling a few stories on what looked to be most interesting and, truthfully, most negative. The positive articles about Trualt and his mission had continued to gain traction, while stories of the Athena force and what they had done were few and far between. I hoped I had enough pull to give the public some balance. As it turned out, I did.

Pentagon remains offline, Athena Force patrolling exterior
World | Oliver Nelms | Washington DC, USA | Wednesday, April 5th, 2124
Athena Force dismantles Chinese nuclear arsenal
World | Oliver Nelms | Beijing, China | Wednesday, April 5th, 2124
European Council being held under Athena Force supervision
World | Oliver Nelms | Brussels, Belgium | Thursday, April 6th, 2124
USS Columbia inert: nuclear submarine crew stranded
Athena Force | Oliver Nelms | Washington DC, USA | Thursday, April 6th, 2124
15 injured in skirmish between Athena Force and Secret Service
Athena Force | Oliver Nelms | Washington DC, USA | Thursday, April 6th, 2124

I did not sleep for the next 40 plus hours. I sat in my hotel room taking calls, watching videos, and reading articles. The situation was stabilizing in some areas and worsening in others. There was so much going on at once, so much information coming to me, I was only able to take in about 10% of what I received. I did my best to find the diamonds in the rough, but that meant ignoring the gold and silver. There was simply too much to report on.

Finally, almost two days after the override, the need for sleep outweighed the need to report, and I went to bed. I did not wake up for almost 20 hours. When I finally opened my eyes, I had a brief moment of doubt, that stereotypical thought process: was it all a dream?

But when I opened my personal, the reality of my new assignment sunk in. The situation was far from over—it had only grown more complex. Meanwhile, my reporting on the Athenas was by and large the most popular. In my time as a journalist I had become moderately well-known, but in those first few days I had catapulted to a level I never imagined possible.

At that point, certain politicians and persons of influence were rallying behind Trualt, and the media continued to push a positive spin. I realized I had an obligation as a journalist to make sure the Athena stories didn't get buried. At the same time, just because I disagreed with what was happening didn't mean I could cherrypick what I was reporting on—I could not become what I was trying to avoid. If my word carried this much weight, I had to do my own research on these growing waves of support for Trualt and the Athenas.

So I stayed in my hotel room studying, reporting, reading, reporting, watching, reporting… This pattern continued for three whole days. I faced a dilemma as a journalist, shutting myself in and not experiencing everything firsthand. But sacrificing this firsthand viewpoint let me see the bigger picture, which, given the volatility of events at that time, I considered more important.

I napped sporadically and the hotel robots brought me my meals. I heard the protests outside, the masses of people increasing in numbers as they realized the Athenas would not attack them. For those three days I continued doing my job, researching and publishing articles on what the military robots were up to.

Gradually, like many others, my own opinion drifted toward the middle. I began to understand what Trualt was saying, to understand what he wanted to do—as I had said, the Earth Initiative was a specific action plan for an idea that had been popular for over twenty years at that point. Most of the public was ready to be convinced. But I tried to keep my opinions out of my reporting. I focused on the Athena force, and let their actions tell the story for me.

TURMOIL IN UN SECURITY COUNCIL AS SUPPORT GROWS FOR ATHENA FORCE
Athena Force | Oliver Nelms | New York City, USA | Saturday, April 8th, 2124
FOUR DEAD AS CHICAGO RIOTS CONTINUE
Athena Force | Oliver Nelms | Chicago, USA | Sunday, April 9th, 2124
ATHENA FORCE HACKS AURORA UNITS
Athena Force | Oliver Nelms | Washington DC, USA | Sunday, April 9th, 2124
ISTANBUL PROTEST TURNS VIOLENT, ATHENA FORCE SUBDUES SEVEN
Athena Force | Oliver Nelms | Istanbul, Turkey | Monday, April 10th, 2124
ATHENA FORCE LAUNCHES RUSSIAN WARHEADS INTO SPACE
Athena Force | Oliver Nelms | Moscow, Russia | Tuesday, April 11th, 2124

After the third day in my room, I had had enough sitting around. I needed to be back on the front line, the only question was where. It was not a shortage of options that was the problem—quite the opposite. There was an abundance of breaking news and I wanted to be everywhere at once. Rather than spend time trying to decide, I went with the most practical route and started right where I was: Paris.

I tried my contacts in the Gendarmerie but they were understandably busy, so I walked in the direction of the most recent Athena sighting.

Even though I had heard the protests from the comfort of my hotel room, seeing the masses of people firsthand made quite the impression. Everyone wanted their opinion on the situation heard. I thought about how different everything had seemed six days earlier, how quiet it had been the night after the override.

Police patrolled the area, some human some not.[5] I knew the human ones were nervous—none of them had their guns on them. But if things got heated, there were more than just police robots around.

After demilitarizing most of the world, a sizable proportion of the Athena force began acting as peacekeepers, supporting the people they

[5] At the time of the override, Paris had over 400 operating humanoid police robots, typically partnered with a human officer. During the override, most of these robots remained in service but the Athena force was able to remotely access them and prevent them from interfering with their mission.

had disarmed. It was a reluctant and uneasy relationship, but police organizations had no choice. No one did.

This has always been the fundamental problem with the entire Earth Initiative: it was not the Earth's decision, it was the decision of Trualt and the Initiators. While there had been growing acceptance and even desire for global unification due to the Robotic Revolution, who was to say this was the proper time and the proper manner to implement it? In all of my articles on the Athena force, I tried to demonstrate this forced reality, this lack of choice. Yes, they made the world better by several metrics, but they never asked the world permission. Again, I leave it to the reader to decide if the ends justified the means.

Back in Paris, it was relatively easy to locate the closest Athena model: anywhere the crowd was dispersed. People had grown brave enough to come out and shout their opinions, but they kept a respectful distance from the military machines. Anyone that got too close might get a stern warning. If they ignored it, they were subdued. Those that pushed the boundaries further were hospitalized.

But very few people fell into the last category. In fact, after talking to several dozen Parisians in my broken French and their perfect English, I learned that most of them were out in support of Trualt. One man even recognized me and called my reporting shameful, saying that I focused on the negative aspects.

I spent the next week covering the Athena force in Paris several hours each day, then returning to my hotel room to catch up on world events. As the Initiator's influence continued to grow, the chaos subsided, slowly but surely.

My articles, while still popular, faded from the center of the spotlight. News about Michael Trualt and the evolving sociopolitical situation took center stage, and the Initiators pushed aggressive social reform with a global agenda. Politicians worldwide argued for or against unity, resigned or were expelled, and governments and economies tried to contend with the unprecedented events unfolding so quickly before them.

A central question that many have tried to answer is how many people knew that the override was coming? There has been no definitive evidence that anyone besides Michael Trualt himself knew what was coming, despite plenty of evidence of his cooperation with hundreds of the Initiators before the override itself. The reason this question is so fascinating is twofold: one, how could people accept such a drastic method and two, how did no one report his plans? The second question alone makes it somewhat plausible that he was in fact the sole person to know exactly what was coming, although that leads to a third question: how could the Initiators play along so quickly when the override occurred?[6]

My colleagues in The Guardian covered these questions as best as they could, but my focus was the Athena force and its relation to the evolving sociopolitical climate. Here again the Initiators deserve a certain level of credit, as the robots were not directly used to pressure individuals—although it would be naive to dismiss their indirect influence on events. This was where my reporting came in: finding the sometimes hidden links between the Athena force and global policy change. To be sure, I still reported on outright confrontations, but these were now relegated to certain zones or the occasional attempted terrorism.

SOMALIAN REPUBLIC CONTINUES TO RESIST ATHENA FORCE
Athena Force | Oliver Nelms | Garowe, Somalian Republic | Thursday, April 13th, 2124
PRESIDENT SHAH DEMANDS TRUALT DISABLE ATHENA FORCE IMMEDIATELY
Athena Force | Oliver Nelms | Washington DC, USA | Friday, April 14th, 2124
FOUR HOSTAGES RESCUED BY ATHENA FORCE IN JERUSALEM
Athena Force | Oliver Nelms | Jerusalem | Saturday, April 15th, 2124
GERMAN MINISTRY OF THE INTERIOR COOPERATING WITH ATHENA FORCE
Athena Force | Oliver Nelms | Berlin, Germany | Sunday, April 16th, 2124
UN GENERAL ASSEMBLY'S "RESISTANCE COALITION" CONDEMNS TRUALT
Athena Force | Oliver Nelms | New York City, USA | Tuesday, April 18th, 2124

[6] For an in-depth investigation into these questions, see *Origins of the Earth Initiative* by Max Sacherin.

Because most of the news from Paris did not require me to actually witness it, I decided it was time to leave. I started a world tour of instability, going places everyone else avoided to see what the Athena force was doing. Many of the nations I visited had already been in political turmoil at the time of the override or had deep-rooted issues that the override had exacerbated. Some were simply digging their heels in, the government openly defying public opinion (at that point, the majority of the population of almost every stable nation was heavily in favor of allowing Trualt to push through his Initiative). In most cases, the Initiators (and by extension, the Athena force) did not try to push any agenda on these hot zones except demilitarization and ceasefires. Unfortunately, these directives were often ignored with deadly results.

CONGO HOSTAGE SITUATION ESCALATES
Athena Force | Oliver Nelms | Lubumbashi, Congo | Monday, April 24th, 2124
CRISIS IN EGYPT CONTINUES: ATHENA FORCE FACES OFFICIAL OPPOSITION
Athena Force | Oliver Nelms | Cairo, Egypt | Tuesday, May 2nd, 2124
ATHENA FORCE SKIRMISH WITH MOSSAD AGENTS LEAVES 12 DEAD
Athena Force | Oliver Nelms | Tel Aviv, Israel | Monday, May 8th, 2124
CIVIL WAR IN SOMALIAN REPUBLIC: ATHENA FORCE DETAINS HUNDREDS
Athena Force | Oliver Nelms | Bosaso, Somalian Republic | Monday, May 15th, 2124
MAJOR SUICIDE BOMBER ATTACK ON ATHENA FORCE: 12 DEAD
Athena Force | Oliver Nelms | Jaipur, India | Sunday, May 21st, 2124

If these deadly results are the 'negative aspects' the Parisian protester was referring to, I think his willingness to dismiss them is misguided. More to the point, Michael Trualt himself claimed the ideals of truth and honesty to be of utmost importance. We should never ignore the side of things that makes us uncomfortable.

Two months after the override, at the beginning of June 2124, I allowed myself a brief family visit in the United States. After my time in the hot zones, the change of pace was surreal. Even President Shah was beginning to acquiesce to the public demands, as Congress was overrun with Initiators pushing their agenda.

I went from watching the Athena force deal with grenades and automatic rifles to rowdy teenagers and belligerent drunks. It was an oddly disconcerting transition. While more and more people rallied behind Trualt and the Initiators, there was always that subconscious understanding, that hidden fear: if he wanted to, he could inflict a lot of damage. Trust in Trualt was growing, but it was not unconditional. Most of that changed with the Fortaleza Suicide.

Of all the continents, South America had perhaps the smoothest transition between the override and the Earth Initiative. After their prosperous resurgence with the Robotic Revolution, most of South America was already converging into the Union of South America, a stronger version of the previous Union of South American Nations that would surpass even the European Union's cohesion. Coupled with the staggering number of Initiators in prominent positions in South American governments, the continent had comparatively little chaos during the years leading up to the Initiative.

Unfortunately, comparatively little was not the same as none. In late June, I started to see stories about a resurgent criminal organization in Brazil known as O Comando. Across the globe, similar groups tried to use the override to their advantage, both as a springboard and a distraction. South America, as mentioned, had been spared a great deal of these resurgences, but O Comando slipped through the cracks. On June 14th, I flew into Rio de Janeiro and began my coverage of the organization's protracted struggle with the Athena force.

O Comando, along with most other criminal and non-criminal resistance groups around the world, knew they could not defeat the Athena force with firepower alone. But once it became clear that Trualt and the Initiators were trying to minimize human harm, these organizations altered their tactics.

Attempts at leverage via hostage negotiations rarely worked. But O Comando tried a novel approach: suicide negotiations. Suicide bombers failed with the Athena force because they were treated as a threat by the robots and treated as terrorists by the media. But getting a hundred people together and threatening, as a group, to commit suicide, all under the guise of fear of robot takeover and the desire to keep your home, keep your family, keep control? That played to the media. Specifically, it played to me.

Yes, the Athena force had access to O Comando's communication avenues and published their plans so we knew this mass suicide was the brainchild of a criminal organization. But 89 people took their own lives, each one convinced by the tumultuous global situation that it was the right choice. O Comando may have persuaded them, but with the state of the world, how hard might that be?

MASS SUICIDE: 89 DEAD IN ATTEMPT TO DISRUPT ATHENA FORCE

Athena Force | Oliver Nelms | Fortaleza, Brazil | Monday, July 10th, 2124

O Comando did not succeed in defeating the Athena force, but they did make one thing very clear: despite the level of calm that had been restored in some areas, there was still unprecedented instability lying beneath the surface. The fact that this happened in South America only deepened the impact.

The Fortaleza Suicide served to emphasize that even when not engaging directly with an enemy, the Athena force posed a threat. My article shot to the top, and the event managed to put a dent in the positive opinion the Initiators had carried thus far.

In response, Michael Trualt visited Fortaleza and personally met with several close family members of the victims. This was his first appearance in a publicly identifiably setting since the override three months prior. Many of the family members refused to meet with him, and of those who did, most openly blamed him for what had happened. There was no press there to report this—Trualt had the interactions shared live for anyone that cared to see.

These interviews, a tactically foolish move even with his contingent of Athena bodyguards,[7] were the key reason the Initiative recovered from the event. Trualt did not argue, did not fight. He apologized, often coming to tears himself, and if given just a moment to speak, would claim to be seeking an end to exactly this type of madness. Again, most of the family members didn't listen. A few got physical, and the Athena models did not intervene.

Whether these interviews were real or staged is a debate that continues to this day. Being in Fortaleza at the time, I can only attest to the mayhem that erupted in the city when news hit of Trualt's presence.

During the interviews, I did my best to ascertain where he was, but I was not the only one trying to track down the most infamous man in the world. The streets were a mess of people. The fact that outright riots did not break out is a testament to the increased Athena presence at the time.

O Comando would go on to attempt several more mass suicide negotiation events, but they were almost universally failures. The organization fell apart a few months later after strategic efforts by the Athena force.

The rest of the year was messy, with pockets of resistance appearing and disappearing around the world, but after the Fortaleza Suicide and Trualt's response, the tide of public opinion truly turned in his favor.

---

[7] According to further reports, the Athena force had to shoot down several inbound strikes during the interviews and disable over 200 covert operatives that tried to converge on the location during the ten hours he was there.

EUROPEAN PARLIAMENT ACCEPTS ATHENA FORCE ACTION IN EU
Athena Force | Oliver Nelms | Brussels, Belgium | Monday, September 25th, 2124
PRESIDENT SHAH OFFICIALLY REINSTATES PERSONAL ATHENA CONTINGENT
Earth Initiative | Oliver Nelms | Washington DC, USA | Saturday, October 14th, 2124
FOUR MORE COUNTRIES WITHDRAW IOC SUITS AGAINST ATHENA FORCE
Earth Initiative | Oliver Nelms | The Hague, Netherlands | Wednesday, November 8th, 2124

The first half of 2125 would see the peak of Trualt's popularity. The Earth Initiative was evolving from an if to a when, a testament to the work of the Initiators. Meanwhile, since the Fortaleza Suicide, news regarding the Athena force faded into the background unless it was directly related to the big picture. In light of the situation, I took a second look at my world tour, revisiting many of the places I had been almost a year earlier.

In some places, Initiative-resistance had evolved from violent to peaceful, but this was rare. What was more common was what I called densification: large areas of moderate resistance had since focused into small pockets of extremity. While this gave the outward appearance of more wide-ranging support, these pockets proved to be a thorn in the Initiative's side: they could not eliminate them, as that would be against their ethics, but they had to contain them, which forced them to bend their ethics anyways.

RESISTANCE FIGHTERS ATTACK UR OUTPOST
Earth Initiative | Oliver Nelms | Mogadishu, Somalian Republic | Friday, January 5th, 2125
TWO ATHENA MODELS DESTROYED BY RESISTANCE FORCES
Earth Initiative | Oliver Nelms | Kazan, Russia | Monday, January 22nd, 2125
RESISTANCE CONTAINMENT ACTION LEAVES 2 DEAD, 23 INJURED
Earth Initiative | Oliver Nelms | Managua, Nicaragua | Sunday, February 18th, 2125

Many of these pockets have had enough resilience to carry on in some form through present day, and these incidents are far from over. But even in 2125, their voice was in the minority, and stability continued to spread.

During my first world tour, I would arrive and report on events firsthand as there was no shortage of daily happenings. On my second round, I usually reported off-site. Of the three headlines above, the closest I got was reaching Mogadishu a few hours after the attack.

On March 1st of 2125, the United Nations formally accepted the Initiative, ushering in a new wave of confidence in Trualt's vision. At that time, public opinion was so positive it was thought the Initiative would take effect at the start of 2126. Of course, this target would end up shifting back by two full years.

The high-level debates among the Initiators and Trualt which prolonged the process began in the summer of 2125, when the Earth Government was brought to public discussion. While this was going on, the Athena force started to reinstate some level of self-sufficiency to specific police forces under the jurisdiction of the United Nations. This was a delicate business, as all but the least lethal weapons were forbidden from being employed. The Athena force was there to take care of the major threats, but Trualt himself said they were meant to be disassembled in the near future. According to him, the decommissioning of the Athena force would be scheduled to coincide with their level of necessity.

This level of necessity turned out to be higher than Trualt anticipated, as no Athena models were officially decommissioned until the very end of 2126. Throughout the back half of 2125 and most of 2126, their main mission was the containment of the aforementioned resilient pockets. As more police units were reinstated, more Athena models dispersed to deal with resistance forces.

Resistance fighters clash with Athena Force outside Dakar
Earth Initiative | Oliver Nelms | Dakar, Senegal | Sunday, July 29th, 2125
Athena Force detains resistance fighters entering Colombia
Earth Initiative | Oliver Nelms | Barranquilla, Colombia | Saturday, September 1st, 2125
Athena model destroyed during raid on resistance forces
Earth Initiative | Oliver Nelms | Ashgabat, Turkmenistan | Tuesday, January 8th, 2126
Athena model disables assassin targeting Initiators
Earth Initiative | Oliver Nelms | Kuala Lumpur, Malaysia | Monday, April 8th, 2126
Resistance fighters clash with Athena Force in Ethiopia
Earth Initiative | Oliver Nelms | Addis Ababa, Ethiopia | Saturday, August 10th, 2126

Despite over a year of fighting, resistance groups failed to make a noticeable dent in the Athena force.[8] While the proportional losses were minimal, each conquered Athena was an urgent problem. If their technology was examined or stolen, it could be a threat to the entire Initiative. For the most part, resistance forces were not successful in commandeering an Athena model, nor were they successful in reverse-engineering any of its advanced weaponry. Their biggest successes were stockpiling ammunition and explosives from the robots.

On three occasions, however, resistance fighters were able to circumvent the sophisticated self-destruct mechanisms and recover a few parts of disabled models. These three occasions marked the most aggressive actions undertaken by the remaining Athena force, and the resistance fighters were quickly stripped of their discoveries.

---

[8] Between the override and the Earth Initiative, only 4011 Athena models (of an original 3,102,454) would be effectively eliminated (approximately 0.13%). Of those, 3289 were eliminated in the first 24 hours after the override, and only 722 more models would meet the same fate in the other 3 years, 8 months, 26 days leading up to the Earth Initiative.

RESISTANCE FIGHTERS IN CHINA DISABLE ATHENA MODEL
Earth Initiative | Oliver Nelms | Qingdao, China | Wednesday, December 20th, 2124
ATHENA MODEL DISABLED IN BRISBANE
Earth Initiative | Oliver Nelms | Brisbane, Australia | Friday, April 13th, 2125
ATHENA MODEL DISABLED BY RESISTANCE FIGHTERS IN SOUTH AFRICA
Earth Initiative | Oliver Nelms | Pretoria, South Africa | Thursday, May 30th, 2126

At the end of 2126, Michael Trualt began the official decommissioning of the Athena force, as promised years before. This was an equally delicate process that required no outside interference. In most cases, Athena models either decommissioned one another or themselves. Once they were sufficiently deconstructed, their raw materials were recycled into new robots by United Robotics, some of which surround us today.

As the Athena force faded into the background, allowing the reinstated police forces to retake the lead, so did my reporting. Some of the hot zones never cooled, but it was clear the world was ready for the Earth Initiative. A precarious balance continued through all of 2127, and less and less Athenas patrolled the streets. The year ended with no major incidents and less violent crime than ever before, another good sign for the Initiators.

On the first day of 2128, the Earth Initiative officially took hold. At 18:00 UTC in New York City, Michael Trualt had his personal escort decommissioned during a well-attended press conference. At 19:14 UTC, just over an hour in, he was killed.

Like the Fortaleza interviews, there are some who claim the entire thing was faked. I know for a fact this is not the case, as I was one of the reporters in the audience.

Michael Trualt was a divisive figure, and his actions were not only illegal, they were deadly. However, his assassination was not justice. Death is never justice, no matter how hard some people would like to believe that.

Paul Fonden, the assassin, was allegedly involved with the resistance, although his motives were likely much more complicated. Whether he was working for himself, for one of the major resistance forces, or perhaps the remnants of some national agency, we will never know for sure.

The one thing I can say with near certainty is Trualt knew what was going to happen. His Athena models were the most sophisticated military advisors in existence, and had likely already learned of the plot via communications analysis. The real question is not why Paul Fonden did what he did, but why Trualt allowed it to happen.

After his assassination, there was a spike in Initiative-resistance activity. This turned out to be an apt test for the new balance of power between the remaining Athena models and Earth's police forces, and they were well up to the cause.

Athena Force helps quell resistance-sparked riots in Poland
Athena | Oliver Nelms | Warsaw, Poland, Earth | Friday, January 2nd, 2128
Athena Force rescues all hostages in Peru
Athena | Oliver Nelms | Lima, Peru, Earth | Friday, January 2nd, 2128
Athena Force clashes with resistance fighters outside Jerusalem
Athena | Oliver Nelms | Jerusalem, Earth | Saturday, January 3rd, 2128

Finally, just over a year after the Earth Initiative took effect, the last Athena model was scheduled for decommissioning. Almost four full years since I got the call for my boss, I wrote my last live article on the military robots.

Final Athena decommissioned: The Athena Force is no more
Athena | Oliver Nelms | New York City, USA, Earth | Friday, March 25th, 2129

At exactly 3:00 pm local time, the final Athena model self-decommissioned in a highly secured ceremony in New York City. After 2 years of multinational service followed by 5 years of Earth service, the Athena force is no more.

For years, the question of whether this day would or could ever come has plagued

> even the most ardent supporters of the Earth Initiative. The Athena force has represented the unfortunate reality of massive social change: no amount of reason will be effective without force.
> This presents a major challenge for our future, but it also presents a major opportunity. Perhaps now is the turning point, the time to leave this unfortunate reality in the past. If we can decommission the need for force just as we have decommissioned the final Athena, their use will not have been in vain.
> Is this a naive plea? Of course. But it is also an optimistic one. Look at how far humanity has come in the past few years. The path forward is open, it is up to us to take it.

At this point I can finally address that which I have thus far completely omitted: the Angel Paradigm. The reason for its prior omission is simple: the Athena force is in direct opposition to the Paradigm itself. Their existence contradicted the Paradigm while simultaneously trying to bring it to fruition. This gave the entire situation a profound irony that should never be ignored.

Most importantly of all, the eradication of the Athena force does not erase its effect on the Paradigm. Within the parameters of the Paradigm there is an implicit assumption that robots do not harm humans. This underlines the irony of the past clearly enough, but it also ignores how that past will affect the future.

Officially, all information pertaining to the Athena has been eradicated beyond retrieval, from the very first blueprint to the very last robot. Their project files were wiped from existence just before the override as corroborated by United Robotics when they first tried to control the situation, and as I have already explained, every attempt to reverse-engineer any of their capabilities has been a failure.

But 3 million robots cannot walk the Earth for seven years and disappear without a trace. Laws can be passed that limit research ventures, hardware and software can be secured in a number of ways, but anything we do is simply a delay. At some point in the future, the technology will reappear. At that point, the question will be what we want to do with it.

This is where I will diverge from my seemingly negative view and propose a compromise. While the Angel Paradigm, as it stands, is not possible, that does not mean the human race is not heading toward a positive future. I believe when the technology reappears, we will not care or need for it—we will have moved on.

The Angel Paradigm assumes humans need robots to guide us to a positive future. In my opinion, we will get there ourselves. The fact the Earth Initiative took hold is testament to that already. As I have underlined before, it was not the Athena force that brought about the Initiative, it was the undercurrent of public support and the strategic actions of the Initiators. Yes, the Athena force was crucial, but it was more of a catalyst, propelling us ahead of schedule to a future I would argue was inevitable.

Of course, now I've lost all objectivity and am digressing into my own opinions. I will stop before I dig too deep of a hole. In summary, I do not believe the Angel Paradigm is our future, but I do believe our future is positive.

I was and continue to be honored that my reporting has made such an impact on this monumental time in history. Thank you all for reading this account, I hope it has been useful in some form or fashion.

10. Colin Lem, Robotist Pastor - - Edited Interview[1]

Pastor Lem is the head of the New York City Robotism Hall, the first church of its kind. He has been a champion of the young religion for over thirty years and was one of the main forces behind its official recognition by the Earth Government and its eventual expansion.

AUTHOR: Hello, Pastor Lem. Thank you for taking the time to be a part of this work.

PASTOR LEM: Of course, Michelle. When I heard about your project, I knew your work was too closely related to our mission to ignore. It should be me thanking you, for spreading the word on the Angel Paradigm.

AUTHOR: Thank you. Pastor Lem, can you explain the core beliefs of Robotism?

PASTOR LEM: Yes. Robotism is quite simple, really. We believe that robots are the path to an idyllic future for humanity: one bereft of violence, prejudice, and hatred. Put simply, we believe in the Angel Paradigm. Don't you?

AUTHOR: Well that depends, Pastor. What exactly is the Angel Paradigm, according to Robotism?

PASTOR LEM: The Angel Paradigm is the final stage of the relationship between humans and robots. It is utopia, in the common sense of the word, wherein robots allow us humans to realize our full potential.

---

[1] Conducted face-to-face 20.11.2133. Pastor Lem asked that the interview remain in a question and answer format. Current form approved by Mr. Lem 30.12.2133.

AUTHOR: Our full potential?

PASTOR LEM: Yes, whatever that may be. No longer will the shackles of society force someone to perform a duty against their will, against their desire. We will be free to realize this full potential.

AUTHOR: When you say a duty against their will, do you mean jobs?

PASTOR LEM: Not necessarily. Perhaps you enjoy what you do. Then with the Angel Paradigm, you continue to do it. But if you don't? You don't have to. The only exception to this is inflicting harm upon others. The Angel Paradigm will not allow this, but it will also remove the desire for this.

AUTHOR: Pastor Lem, are you saying that through the Angel Paradigm, humans will no longer wish harm on one another?

PASTOR LEM: I know, it sounds like typical religious quackery. But I assure you it is true. Just look at what we have now with robot teachers: mortality formation.[2] This is the first step of many in which the human condition is cleansed of its selfishness. As I said, the Paradigm is the final stage.

AUTHOR: Pastor, many people have trouble understanding what makes Robotism a religion. Could you explain it in your own words?

PASTOR LEM: Yes. Robotism is a belief system without rituals or ceremonies, only faith. We put our faith in robots, not humans. As humans ourselves, it is our duty to do our part to allow the robots to save us. This is the key mission of Robotism.

---

[2] Morality formation is covered in more detail by Dr. Kyle Fix (chapter 7).

AUTHOR: You say you are a religion without ceremonies. In that case, what do you do at your church?

PASTOR LEM: As you know, we do not refer to it is a church, simply a hall. And that is what it is—a meeting place. A place for likeminded people to interact and share, or to bring in skeptics and explain our views.

AUTHOR: If it is a hall, and not a church, why do you take the title of pastor?

PASTOR LEM: An entirely cultural choice, to be honest. The term pastor evokes both authority and piety, something we decided was appropriate for the head members. It's nothing more than a formality.

AUTHOR: Pastor Lem, there are many people who agree with the main message of Robotism: that the Angel Paradigm is the future, that robots will bring us to utopia, etcetera. But they do not call themselves Robotists. What defines a Robotist beyond these core beliefs?

PASTOR LEM: Truthfully, not much. In fact, many of these people you mention are probably Robotists, whether they use the label or not. If someone truly believes robots are the key to humanity's future, and if they believe in the pure form of the Angel Paradigm—one of utopia guided by the robots—then they are a Robotist.

AUTHOR: And if these Robotists also prescribe to another religion?

PASTOR LEM: Then they are welcome to do so. We do not have a jealous deity or a sternly worded tome from eons ago. We have science and reality. But as I said before, we also have faith. Because faith is needed for the path ahead, faith and action based on it. We do not trust some god to push us in the right direction, but we do trust the robots.

AUTHOR: Would you go so far as to call the robots gods?

PASTOR LEM: That is a matter of semantics. A god as in Christianity or Islam? Certainly not. But one of the definitions of the word god is as follows: a superhuman being or spirit worshipped as having power over nature or human fortunes. In this case, maybe a robot is a god. It is a superhuman being after all, and it has power over nature and human fortunes. But is it worshipped? Now we reach a second layer of semantics. Worshipped as in adored or revered? Yes, but we have to be careful here. As with any religion, worship can lead down a dark path, a path contrary to the peaceful and loving utopia the Angel Paradigm wishes to bring about. But this is a tale as old as time. In the end I would answer your question with maybe. The word god is such a powerful one and the role of robots is so complex that it would be unfair to give a concrete response. My apologies.

AUTHOR: Not at all, although I will continue this line of thought: who guides this utopian future, robots or humans?

PASTOR LEM: Again I am faced with a semantic trap. What do you mean by 'guides'? In the end, the future is for humanity, but it is shaped by robots. This is another reason it would be a mistake to call them gods. We are not serving them.

AUTHOR: Are you saying the robots should decide our future?

PASTOR LEM: To an extent, yes. For the time being, this is impossible. We do not have robots capable—humans still make almost all of the decisions. But in the future, they should pave the path to utopia, and we shall walk it.

AUTHOR: Pastor Lem, how do we know the robots will pave a path to utopia? After all, for the time being as you said, humans make most of the decisions. How do we know when it is time to hand over the reins, so to speak?

PASTOR LEM: An excellent question without an answer, at this point. My apologies once more. This is simply something we will have to recognize when the time comes.

AUTHOR: But if humans guide the evolution of robots, isn't it possible we miss the Angel Paradigm completely? Isn't it possible robots evolve in a more malicious manner?

PASTOR LEM: Ah, yes. This is a real concern—the real concern. That is what Robotism stands for today: guiding the humans so that eventually, we can be guided by the robots. We are working to make sure the Angel Paradigm remains the top priority in robot development, so that once their intelligence rises, they are already imbued with altruism and peace.

AUTHOR: How exactly does Robotism guide the evolution of robots today?

PASTOR LEM: Politically. When we congregate in our hall, it is to discuss our political plan of action. We make an effort to contact persons of influence in the world of robotics, and have had a few of them join our movement. The more we convert, the better.

AUTHOR: Are you saying you target certain people and try to convert them?

PASTOR LEM: For the third time I'm afraid I disagree with your word choice. Target has a very aggressive connotation. We actively seek out roboticists and legislators and have open and meaningful discussions with them. I also wouldn't say we try to convert anyone. In most cases, an individual realizes that they are a Robotist, even if they hadn't used the label—as I mentioned before. I've had dozens of people come into this hall a skeptic, sit in that same chair you're sitting in right now, and after a lengthy conversation, they leave this hall a Robotist.

AUTHOR: Pastor Lem, going back a bit: you mentioned that at some point, we hand over our destiny to the robots, is that correct?

PASTOR LEM: In a manner of speaking, yes. We write the code, we lay the foundation for where we are headed, but at a certain point we let go of the wheel.

AUTHOR: Yes. Now this transition, you said, will come at an unknown point, a point where the robots have reached a certain higher level of intelligence, correct?

PASTOR LEM: Correct.

AUTHOR: What happens if the intelligence gains consciousness? Are they still our agents of utopia?

PASTOR LEM: Before I answer, may I pose a related question to you?

AUTHOR: Yes, go ahead.

PASTOR LEM: If robots gain a consciousness, is the Angel Paradigm still possible?

AUTHOR: In my opinion, in the way it is understood today, no.

PASTOR LEM: I agree. And Robotism agrees. It is our position that robots will never gain consciousness. Only time will tell.

AUTHOR: Do you hold that robots will continue to gain intelligence, or are you saying they will reach a ceiling?

PASTOR LEM: I do not believe they will reach a ceiling. I also do not think a conscience is a natural product of an increasing intelligence. I think it is something far more complex and, dare I say, special. If you allow me to use an old analogy, robots will grow in their intelligence until we are but ants in their eyes. But if the foundation of this intelligence is rooted in keeping those ants healthy, happy, and devoting themselves to these ants, then the Angel Paradigm will continue forever.

AUTHOR: Pastor Lem, your analogy brings up a good point: wouldn't it be a waste for such a vast intelligence to take care of us? Wouldn't it be a waste for the human race to care for ants?

PASTOR LEM: This is a common argument, and I understand where you are coming from. But I go back to what I said about a conscience. We are a unique species with a unique gift. Though our intellect may not match the robots of the future—or today's robots, really—we are still worth the effort.

AUTHOR: So humans are more important than robots?

PASTOR LEM: Always. We may think of robots as angels, but we do not worship them, as I have stressed before. The Angel Paradigm is fundamentally about humans and our future, and so is Robotism.

AUTHOR: If I may, Pastor Lem, I'd like to move to one last subject.

PASTOR LEM: Of course, Michelle.

AUTHOR: Thank you. What is Robotism's position on cyborgs, androids, and biorobotics in general?

PASTOR LEM: A bit vague, but only because it is such a broad and dynamic field. Human enhancement at its current level does not really affect Robotism. These individuals are still very much human and their path remains the same as our own. As far as making robots more humanlike, this is neither required nor forbidden by the Angel Paradigm so, in essence, it is effectively not an issue. You could say we are neutral. However, there is one exception: a robot being so humanlike that it cannot be distinguished from a human, what I call a 'perfect android.' The perfect android is a threat to the Angel Paradigm. Now this perfect android, as I have argued, would not have a conscience, but its outward appearance, mannerisms, speech patterns… every little physical detail would replicate a human with such accuracy that we would not be able to tell the difference. Why is a perfect android a threat to the Angel Paradigm? Because it can become an imposter in the human side of the equation. A robot treated like a human when it is a being without a conscience brings up some ethical questions. It throws off the proper order of things in the Angel Paradigm, do you understand?

AUTHOR: Can you elaborate?

PASTOR LEM: Certainly. If there is an android impersonating a human so well that even humans cannot tell the difference, but this being has no consciousness, we lose the very foundation of the Paradigm: that humans, as beings with a conscience, are unique, and that our future at the hands of the robots is meant for us and us alone. These robots will not have emotions or feelings, they will be no more than highly sophisticated computers. Their job is to serve us, even as they guide us. Does that explain it better?

AUTHOR: Yes, Pastor Lem, thank you.

PASTOR LEM: This is another, smaller endeavor we are undertaking: to make sure such an android does not come to pass, to standardize some measure, some way of making sure a robot is in fact a robot. For the foreseeable future this is not an issue, a pocket metal detector can quickly sense the difference. But if cerebral units give way to biorobotic brains? It's a tricky subject.

AUTHOR: Thank you, Pastor Lem. I appreciate your willingness to contribute to my project.

PASTOR LEM: Of course, Michelle. Best of luck, and remember: the Angel Paradigm is the future. We must embrace it. You are welcome in our hall any time.

11. Rita Berge, Cognitive Scientist - - Edited Excerpt[1]

Dr. Berge is a cognitive scientist working as a consultant for United Robotics. Her knowledge of the basic tenants of what is known as the philosophy of artificial intelligence gives insight into the complex world of robot intelligence.

Cognitive science is the study of the mind and its processes. This is, of course, quite a broad field of study, covering many mental faculties. Reasoning, emotion, language, perception, attention, and memory are all part of the mind and its processes. This vast expanse of knowledge overlaps several other fields, including neuroscience, psychology, linguistics, philosophy, and anthropology.

All of these faculties and all of these fields have implications in the study of artificial intelligence. And since the Angel Paradigm is based on artificial intelligence, it is important to understand robotic minds and their processes in order to understand the Angel Paradigm itself.

The three major questions in AI today are as follows:

1) *Can a machine be intelligent?*
2) *Are machine intelligence and human intelligence fundamentally different?*
3) *Can a machine have consciousness?*

Whether any of these questions can be answered definitively with present knowledge is up for debate. There are a number of conjectures and ideas grounded in scientific fact that aim to at least begin the process of answering them. What follows is an attempt to explain these arguments in a manner that is accessible to the reader.

---

[1] Adapted from her book *AI: The Science of Robot Intelligence.* Dr. Berge has edited several sections together to give a concise primer on the science behind artificial intelligence. She has also graciously added her thoughts on the Angel Paradigm. Current form approved by Dr. Berge 17.02.2134.

Before delving into these subjects, a prerequisite question must be answered, namely:

What is a machine?

A dictionary gives the following definition:

machine /məˈʃiːn/ noun
an apparatus using mechanical power and having several parts, each with a definite function and together performing a particular task.

All robots are machines but not all machines are robots. This may seem like a basic distinction, but when dealing with the aforementioned three questions, it is important to stay as precise as possible in our language, particularly because the questions themselves are quite broad. The first is arguably broadest of all:

1) *Can a machine be intelligent?*

In order to answer this question, another word must be defined: intelligence.

intelligence /ɪnˈtɛlɪdʒ(ə)ns/ noun
the ability to acquire and apply knowledge and skills.

Therefore, can an apparatus using mechanical power and having several parts, each with a definite function and together performing a particular task, have the ability to acquire and apply knowledge and skills?

This is already a mouthful, but the truth of the matter is it only gets worse. Looking at the question now, one may be tempted to answer yes. After all, many robots have the ability to acquire and apply knowledge and skills. But there is an assumption in this supposition: one's understanding of the words acquire and apply.

What does it mean to acquire and apply knowledge? After all, it could be argued that a thermostat acquires knowledge (the ambient temperature) and applies it (increase or decrease temperature). Is a thermostat intelligent?

Again, one may answer yes. That is not the right answer, nor is it the wrong one. The problem lies with the definition of intelligence: it cannot be objective enough to give a final verdict. In the end, however, the answer to the first question is almost certainly yes.

If one does not agree that a thermostat is intelligent, then what about a self-driving car? And if not a self-driving car, what about a robot? At some iteration of machine complexity, almost the entire spectrum of the definition of intelligence will be satisfied.

1) *Can a machine be intelligent?*

Answer: Depending on the definition of intelligence, almost certainly yes.

There is, however, one case where the answer is almost certainly no: when intelligence is defined as human intelligence, including all the nuance of the human mind. This leads to the second question:

2) *Are machine intelligence and human intelligence fundamentally different?*

The astute reader will realize that semantics plays a role here as well: what does it mean to be fundamentally different? Rather than cite the dictionary, however, a clever solution can be proposed: if the human brain could be simulated, then there would exist a machine intelligence precisely matching a human intelligence. Ergo, there would be no fundamental difference. As it turns out, there are two major problems with the 'artificial brain' approach.

First, complete simulation of the brain is still not possible. For decades, scientists have understood and yet underestimated the complexity of our body's control center. The human brain contains almost a hundred billion neurons, each complex and variable.[2] Each of these neurons in turn connects to thousands of other neurons via synapses. Each synapse is made of over 1000 different proteins, and are themselves dynamic, changing. All of these components adapt to electrical and chemical inputs —hormones, for example—and each one adapts differently.

These layers of complexity have made the artificial brain elusive.[3] Perhaps there exists a threshold of complexity that needs to be simulated after which the model is self-correcting, but this threshold has not been reached.

The second major problem with the artificial brain is the theory of embodied cognition: in essence, human intelligence is shaped by more than just the brain. Even if a true simulation of the human brain were possible, it would still not have a human intelligence because it lacks interaction with an environment.[4]

So the clever solution is not yet a viable one. But there already exists a well-developed technology that is as close as science has gotten to the artificial brain: the cerebral unit.

Cerebral units are not simulations of human brains, but they do borrow heavily from that line of research. Perhaps this is the better avenue to

---

[2] For example, axons have differing transmission speeds. In addition, dendrite shape and molecular composition affect sensitivity to synaptic input.

[3] Current brain simulations focus on one or more facets of this complexity. These simulations have been profoundly useful in the fields of neuroscience, cognitive science, linguistics, and robotics.

[4] An interesting corollary to this is Moravec's Paradox: high-level reasoning requires little computation while low-level sensorimotor skills require enormous computation. It is interesting to consider what this implies about the human brain, human intelligence, and machine intelligence.

machine intelligence; after all, early flying machines were based on birds, but modern airplanes do not look like pigeons.

Returning to the issue at hand, is the machine intelligence of a robot with a cerebral unit fundamentally different from the human intelligence of a person with a brain? At this point it may be tempting to say yes, but why?

One proposed fundamental difference between human intelligence and machine intelligence is true understanding of input. Current cerebral units pass several iterations of the Turing test with ease,[5] but do the machines *understand* the questions being posed to them, or are they simply *simulating* understanding? For a clever explanation, compare human language acquisition to robot language acquisition:

Consider an adult human who speaks one language and begins to learn another. In the beginning, this person will likely translate words or phrases and follow basic grammar rules. This is similar to a language program put in a robot, with given inputs and outputs based on specified patterns.

At first, a human may know the direct translation of 'how are you?' so that when it is heard, their brain translates the question then searches for the translations of 'good' or 'bad' in order to answer. This can be argued as a simulation of understanding: the person does not truly understand the language, they are still translating into their original language to answer the question. But at some point, the human will truly understand the language, and 'how are you?' will no longer follow this pre-determined path.

What about the robot? While it is true that every input will be 'translated' to the robot's source code in order to provide an output, a cerebral unit's code is very advanced. A response to 'how are you?' will not simply be a choice of several unique outputs: evolutionary algorithms, fuzzy logic, machine learning… all of these aspects of soft computing give the robot the ability to conduct natural and fluent conversations.

---

[5] Numerous studies have shown that humans cannot tell the difference between human-generated and robot-generated responses for robots with current-model cerebral units when the responses are presented as text on a screen with no indication of their origin.

It could be argued that all of these sophisticated processes taking place within the cerebral unit are simply the machine versions of the processes taking place in human brains. A human understands and a machine understands, and in the end both speak a language fluently. Even when a human truly understands something, in the end it is only a combination of neurons firing. Source code and firing neurons can be argued to be 'fundamentally different,' but if they both reach the same conclusion, does it matter?

In the end, this is not the question that has been posed. Whether or not machine intelligence and human intelligence are fundamentally different depends on how human intelligence is defined. If it is simply being able to answer questions like a human, then there is no fundamental difference. But if it includes all the nuance of the human mind, as well as its physical architecture, then the fundamental difference is there.

2) Are machine intelligence and human intelligence fundamentally different?

Answer: Depending on the definition of human intelligence, most likely yes.

Notice that the answer to the second question is not as strong as the answer to the first. One of the ways to resolve both of these questions is by answering the third:

3) Can a machine have consciousness?

Typically, 'all the nuance of the human mind' means consciousness. If having a conscience is considered a requirement for human intelligence, then the answer to the second question is yes—there is a fundamental difference between machine intelligence and human intelligence, even without considering the neurons versus the code. But if a machine were able to have a conscience, it could then be argued that machine intelligence and human intelligence are not fundamentally different for most definitions of human intelligence (excepting those dependent on the physical properties of the brain itself). Unfortunately, there is once again a vague set of words posing an obstacle: what does it mean to have consciousness?

There is no agreed upon definition of consciousness. Self-awareness, sentience, subjectivity: each of these subsets of consciousness is equally hard to define. Whether machines have any of these qualities in any form is up for debate.

Another issue arises from the second question. If machine intelligence is fundamentally different from human intelligence, is consciousness even possible? Can the processes and architecture within a cerebral unit bring about consciousness, or is it a unique product of the processes and architecture of the brain?

For the time being, while cerebral units borrow from artificial brain research, they do little in terms of human brain simulation.[6] Meanwhile, roboticists have separated the independent morality problem from consciousness, arguing that the former can be programmed while the latter cannot (at least for the time being). But even if cerebral units diverge more and more from human brains, will they evolve a new type of consciousness, similar but different to our own?

The arguments here are less scientific and more philosophical. In the end, the answer is very clearly not clear at all:

3) Can a machine have consciousness?

Answer: Depending on the definition of consciousness, perhaps.

A terrible answer, but it should come as no surprise. Now, how do the answers to these questions affect the Angel Paradigm?

---

[6] This depends on the manufacturer and model. Some companies are actively pursuing 'brain mirroring' in cerebral units, which is to say an architecture and processes that more closely simulate the human brain.

The first question is critical. If a machine cannot be intelligent, it certainly cannot be entrusted with safeguarding the human race. The Angel Paradigm itself is not well-defined, but depending on how much control is handed over, machine intelligence would not only need to exist, it would need to be of a magnitude greater than humanity's.

The second question is also critical. If machine intelligence and human intelligence are fundamentally different, what happens when machine intelligence surpasses humanity's ability to understand it? A machine intelligence that cannot be understood is one that likely cannot be controlled, and this could stop the Angel Paradigm in its tracks. Inversely, if machine intelligence and human intelligence are fundamentally the same, a consciousness will likely emerge in the future, leading to the third question.

The third question is naturally just as critical as the first two. If a machine develops consciousness, the Angel Paradigm no longer exists in its current form. In this situation, the possibilities are too complex and beyond current understanding to give any sort of relevant assessment of what might occur. Do machines possess the same consciousness as humans, and if not, how is it different? Does machine consciousness exclude the possibility of the Angel Paradigm, or does it simply alter its meaning?

These questions are even more complicated than the three considered herein and are left for the future cognitive scientists, neuroscientists, roboticists, and philosophers to ponder. Good luck.

12. Maria Castaño, Ecologist - - Edited Presentation[1]

Dr. Castaño is an ecological researcher in the Earth Department of the Environment. Her research into social and cultural anthropology and their relation to the environment presents a unique view of the ecological effects, current and future, of the Angel Paradigm.

There is no doubt about it: humans have abused Earth for hundreds of years. We are an unprecedented global superpredator, disrupting the delicate checks and balances of the planetary ecosystem. At present, the rate of extinction of species is estimated to be about 10,000 times higher than the 'natural' rate, or what would be historically typical without the influence of humanity. Climate change continues to threaten our very existence, despite the strong preventative measures we have taken over the past century.

The problem is the environmentalist movement is weak compared to the economic appetite for our planet's resources. From a strictly scientific point of view, this isn't all too surprising. Our brains are hard-wired for short-term gain; we are simple animals in need of energy and on the quest to reproduce. But evolution has gifted us with an intelligence that can sometimes look past this hard-wiring, an intelligence that allows us to consider the long-term.

Looking into the long-term has brought about several interesting propositions. Ironically (and unfortunately), long-term thinking tends to be short-term itself: every decade we have a new idea for the next century. Right now, the philosophy of the day is the Angel Paradigm. Whether it will stand the test of time remains to be seen, but we need to be prepared in the case that it does. At this point you may wonder, what does the Angel Paradigm have to do with ecology? As it turns out, lots.

---

[1] Adapted from her presentation *Robots & the Environment: The Future of Machines, Humans, and Earth.* Current form approved by Dr. Castaño 02.02.2134.

I like to call myself an anthropological ecologist. This is distinct from the more common ecological anthropologist. They study cultural adaptations to environments. I study environmental adaptations to cultures. For example, how does the current trend of robotization and automation of labor affect our planet? What does the increased presence of robots mean for the environment? More generally, what does the Angel Paradigm mean for the environment? You may be surprised by the answers.

In general, the automation of labor has had a net positive effect on the environment. Machines tend to be more efficient than humans. For example, self-driving vehicles (commercial and private) are significantly more efficient than their human counterparts, saving on fuel (most run renewably, but the fact remains), space (no need for a cockpit), and materials. But what about robots?

Steel and aluminum are the main robot-building materials, and thank goodness. Almost 100% of both of these materials are recycled by the robotics industry, dismantling older models to create newer ones. That is not to say robot construction has no environmental impact, but with an almost perfect record of reusable energy sources and highly regulated, environmentally friendly practices oftentimes made easier by the use of the robots themselves, the robotics industry remains remarkably clean.

In fact, robots have been particularly useful in several environmental programs, from national park upkeep to chemical spill cleanup. One notable effect of robotic proliferation is the rise of the sustainable agriculture model, with an extremely low ecological footprint. Robots act as local farmers for small communities, creating short food supply chains with almost no packaging or food processing. Even meat, which is now almost 100% lab-grown, is decreasing its ecological footprint.[2]

[2] Cultured meat has decreased the energy needs of the meat industry by almost 50%, and coupled with vertical farming, it has lowered the land use for the meat industry dramatically: the total land area used by the meat industry in 2130 is 4% of what it was in 2050.

Okay, case closed, robots are awesome, let's pat ourselves on the back and we're good to—

No, not quite. We haven't talked about the Angel Paradigm yet.

I know what you're thinking: the Angel Paradigm? How could that be bad for the environment? Well, it might be or it might not be. It really depends on what path we end up following.

First I should mention I will take the Angel Paradigm in its most common form: robots will lead to a successful future for humanity. But what does success mean for humanity? I repeat: we are simple animals in need of energy and on the quest to reproduce. I'd rather not talk about how robots can help with the second part (you can use your imagination on that one), but I do want to talk about the first.

If the Angel Paradigm comes to pass, I am certain humans will live longer, healthier lives. These lives will also be much more comfortable, allowing them the opportunity to bear offspring, if they so choose, without any of the usual obstacles. You can see where this is going.

The Angel Paradigm will immediately exacerbate the already prominent issue of human overpopulation. This poor planet of ours was not meant to harbor this many of us, that much is frighteningly clear. What happens if we have a population explosion thanks to our newfound prosperity?

The first response is that the Angel Paradigm will avoid this eventuality, as the robots will realize that overpopulation can threaten the Paradigm itself. That is unlikely. The robots telling us to stop having babies? I don't see that going over well.

What is more likely is the robots will use their super intellect to come up with some super solution we haven't come up with yet. Or maybe just use the best one we have now: space colonization.

Space colonization is an inevitability for our species. Again, there is simply no way Earth can handle us for another million years. Realistically, we probably only have a tenth of that, or even a hundredth. Is space colonization viable in the next 10,000 years?

Admittedly, this is not my field of expertise, but I am a curious anthropological ecologist, so I did some research. The consensus? Yes, most likely we will be able to reach into the stars and make new homes before we run out of time.[3]

That's good news. But I have one caveat: this is not an excuse for us to trash our home. Earth created us, shaped us, raised us. We have to respect her as best as we can, even as we plan for the future. In the best case scenario, we are able to leave her before it is too late and she is able to heal. In my whimsical fantasy, Earth becomes a sort of museum, a piece of art if you will. Our home is left to do as she pleases, and we watch from the sidelines in awe.

And what of these new worlds, these colonies? There is an ethical consideration to planetary terraforming. By most measures, we will have to make some adjustments to the planet's ecology in order to survive as a species. Just because these planets are not Earth, are we entitled to make changes to their environment? The level of terraforming will depend on the planet in question and the technological and economical feasibility of the project, but the fact remains: even if we found a perfect Earth clone, simply setting foot on it would change the ecology.

Clearly we need to find a balance that acknowledges our desire for survival while implementing measures to preserve the alien ecosystem. After all, we wouldn't want some other advanced race to arrive at Earth and go about drying our oceans or pumping our atmosphere full of sulphur just because they wanted some new alien condos.

There is one other solution I have purposefully left for the end because it is both a bit further in our future (more so than space colonization, in my opinion), and not necessarily as effective for our planet: human uploading. What I mean by that is the ability to upload our entire self—consciousness and all—into a virtual reality running on a machine. With the help of robots, we may even be able to upload the entire human

[3] See *Beyond Earth* by Sophie Ely for a look at the future of space colonization and robots.

species onto some sort of virtual platform the robots can then maintain. A platform such as this would not be a major superpredator. Its environmental footprint would by all accounts be much smaller than ours has been. And win-win, in our virtual reality we can waste all the resources we want because they are infinite!

Clearly this is reaching, but it is also related to the Angel Paradigm. In a simulation like this, humans may truly be free to be happy, with no repercussions whatsoever. Perhaps space colonization will come first, but looking thousands of years into the future, something like this becomes more and more probable. Will the human race one day exist outside the physical realm? What if someone pulls the plug? Since this is such a fanciful hypothesis, I will leave those questions open.

So yes, I do concede that if the Angel Paradigm includes the eventual colonization of space and/or some super intelligent solution that spares our planet, it is not a threat. And I would assume that by the very definition of the Angel Paradigm, it would avoid destroying Earth. But one can never be sure. If we focus just on human prosperity, this can be achieved in a number of ways that do not take the environment into account. I want to be sure that we do. It's the least we can do for Earth, especially after all we've done to her. Don't you think?

13. Isabel Marotto, Enhanced Athlete - - Unedited Interview[1,2]

Isabel Marotto is a professional enhanced footballer who plays as a forward for Italy in the IFEF.[3] She has been the team captain for seven seasons. Her rise to stardom and her record as a cyborg equality activist has brought the enhanced athlete debate to the forefront of the sporting world.

AUTHOR: Good evening, Isabel.

ISABEL: Ciao, Michelle. How are you?

AUTHOR: Well, thank you. And you?

ISABEL: Also well.

AUTHOR: Isabel, I know we have corresponded about my project, so I will jump right to it. My first question is a popular one: what do you think of the term cyborg? Do you prefer to be called a cyborg athlete, or an enhanced one?

ISABEL: Ah, yes. The naming is an issue for some people. Me, not so much. I know cyborg is usually seen as a bad word, almost like a racist word. That is why everywhere you see the word enhanced. But enhanced is not a very good word—it is not very specific. Enhanced athletes have existed for over a hundred years, before cyborgs they were— the word was

---

[1] Conducted via video/audio chat 04.09.2133. Ms. Marotto asked that the interview remain unedited. After further correspondence, I was given permission to remove most fillers (e.g. um, uh, er). Current form approved by Ms. Marotto 20.12.2133.

[2] Author's note: this section has admittedly less to do with the Angel Paradigm than most, but I have left it as it sheds light onto another facet of robotics that plays into the greater picture of the Paradigm.

[3] International Federation of Enhanced Football

for drugs. And drugs were always cheating. But cyborgs? We have our own league. We are not cheating.

AUTHOR: So to you, cyborg isn't necessarily an offensive term?

ISABEL: No, why would it be? It is what I am. It is what? Robot and organic?[4] That is what we are. Enhanced is too vague.

AUTHOR: Yes, and as you say, in the past it had to do with drugs and cheating. What about today? Isn't it true that cyborg enhancements give an unfair advantage?

ISABEL: Against normal humans it would be unfair, yes. But like I said, we have our own league.

AUTHOR: The IFEF.

ISABEL: Yes, IFEF. All footballers in IFEF are cyborgs.

AUTHOR: How does IFEF decide what is allowed? Are there rules about certain enhancements?

ISABEL: No, no there are none. There are none because there is a limit — cyborgs cannot be ten times as fast as a human, or ten times as powerful. The human body cannot take that level of stress. Remember, all of our enhancements are still based on our natural body. Everything is connected to our normal organs and skin. If we try to make our kick too strong, we will take out our leg.

AUTHOR: So there are no limits in the rules, but there are limits based on biomechanics?

ISABEL: Yes, exactly.

---

[4] Cyborg is short for cybernetic organism, a being with both organic and biomechatronic parts.

AUTHOR: Do you think some cyborgs are more enhanced than others, putting them at an advantage?

ISABEL: That is a hard question. I know some players are better than others, but it is the same in the normal leagues. How much of a cyborg is just talent? People ignore that because they see the enhancements, you know?

AUTHOR: I understand. And you, can you tell us why you decided to enhance yourself?

ISABEL: Ha, yes. It was a simple decision. I was in an accident when I was younger. 16. My legs were paralyzed, but I had already fallen in love with football. The doctors said they might be able to give me my feeling back, but it would take a long time and I would never be one hundred percent. I said no, just give me cyborg legs. So they did the switch.

AUTHOR: Are you happy with your decision?

ISABEL: Yes, very. I was able to play again after a few months. I got used to the legs. One year later, I was on Italy's preparation squad for IFEF.

AUTHOR: You are a cyborg equality activist. Could you explain in your own words what that means?

ISABEL: Yes. First, I want to remind people that cyborgs are not new. People have had hearing aids, heart pace machines, or BCIs for many, many years. What is happening now is robotic arms and legs are less expensive. For me, I did not really need these legs, but I decided I want them and so I got them. This is what makes people angry. They say it is not natural. There are a lot of rules about who can do it and who can't. If I didn't have my accident, I could not just go to a doctor and tell them to replace my legs. Not in a legal— not legally. But even though I did it legally, I still make people angry. They tell me I should have let my legs heal naturally. Why? It is my body, it is my choice.

AUTHOR: Do you think people should be able to get enhancements as they please? Even without a medical reason?

ISABEL: Yes. Why not? People are scared, they are jealous. But it is like a tattoo or a piercing. It is a way to express yourself, to be different. Wheelchairs are not needed anymore, but still people say that is the right way to go. That is crazy! They want someone to never walk again instead of being able to walk normally, just because they are scared.

AUTHOR: I understand why you think people might be jealous, but why do you think they might be scared?

ISABEL: Well it is true, my kick is very strong *(laughs)*. Strong enough to hurt people. But a normal kick can hurt people too. It is like a weapon, I guess, but I do not use it like that.

AUTHOR: Do you think there are parallels between biorobotics and genetic engineering?

ISABEL: I don't understand.

AUTHOR: Do you think there are similarities between cyborg enhancements and genetic enhancements?

ISABEL: Ah, yes. Another debate! Genetic enhancements are similar because they are also enhancements, but those are made without the person's choice, before they are born. I think that issue is more complicated than ours. If you ask someone if they should be able to remove some terrible disease, they usually say yes. But what about just a small chance of it, or if it is not that terrible? Then when they talk about eye color and things like that—you know, physical things—they always say no, that is too far. But that is silly. Everyone knows that looks matter. If you can make someone look better, they will almost always be more successful in life. That might be even more important than that disease! So that is a very complex issue. Yes, it is similar, but more complicated. Good question.

AUTHOR: So would you argue that cybernetic enhancements that are purely superficial, just for looks, should be allowed?

ISABEL: Yes, that is what I would say. For the same reasons as the genetic ones. If I can make my face or body more attractive, I should have the choice because it does affect our lives. People want to say that it doesn't but it does. It always did and it always will.

AUTHOR: Thank you, Isabel. I want to make a quick detour to the subject of my book. Do you know about the Angel Paradigm?

ISABEL: Yes, it is a very popular thing.

AUTHOR: Do you think cyborgs change the Angel Paradigm at all?

ISABEL: Hm, that is another good question. In the future, our options will become more complicated, like the genetics. At some point I think we will have a cyborg that is more robot than human, and then what do we call them? If I put a human brain in a robot today, what is that? A human or a robot?

AUTHOR: What would you say it was?

ISABEL: A human. The brain is human, the soul is human. That is why I think that even if I replaced all my body parts with machine, I would still be a human.

AUTHOR: So how would that affect the Angel Paradigm?

ISABEL: If you agree with me and say that they are still a human, I think it doesn't change it. The Angel Paradigm is still the same. The robots, the ones without human souls, continue to be robots.

AUTHOR: Do you think the opposite can happen, that a robot can develop a consciousness and become human?

ISABEL: I… do not think so. I think also the problem is, what is consciousness? What is a soul? I believe these are things only humans can have. I do not think you can program them.

AUTHOR: Never? You think it will never be possible?

ISABEL: No, never.

AUTHOR: In that case, do you think the Angel Paradigm is going to happen?

ISABEL: I think if robots had souls the Angel Paradigm would not happen. But without souls, I don't know. I hope so, but I am worried. Robots are still controlled by humans. We have to find a balance, where we do not control them directly, but we know they will do what is best for us. And I do not know if that balance is possible. I do not know if you can have one without the other.

AUTHOR: You say that a robot cannot have a soul, but you also say a human brain in a robot body is a human. Do you think this will happen in the future? Do you think cyborgs will replace humans?

ISABEL: I think eventually, yes. This is the next stage of our evolution. Right now there is fear and jealousy, as I said, but there is always fear and jealousy at the beginning. In one hundred years, things will be different. In one thousand years, maybe normal humans won't exist anymore.

AUTHOR: Do you think that humans could become too robotic? With BCIs or maybe virtual reality, do you think we could lose our souls?

ISABEL: Wow, I have never thought about that. But you know what, I think you are right. I think that might be possible. That is very scary. Ha! See, now I am afraid. But I don't know if that is a good change. That is a good question, it makes me understand a little better why people are afraid of cyborgs. Maybe I have been wrong this whole time! *(laughs)*

AUTHOR: It was a pleasure speaking with you, Isabel. Thank you for your time and good luck this season.

ISABEL: *(laughs)* Thank you, Michelle. You have made me think about things that I did not think about before. I hope that I was able to answer your questions. I cannot wait to see the book when it is finished.

14. Jacqueline Lepperin, Court Justice - - Edited Interview[1]

Dr. Lepperin is a Justice of the European Supreme Court and a former Initiator. She was heavily involved in the formation of what would become the Earth Court system and was one of the most outspoken adversaries of Trualt's Robotic Assembly Proposal.

The Earth Government is one of the most astounding successes of the Earth Initiative. In its seven years of existence, it has managed to reach a level of legitimacy even I would not have anticipated. What many people do not realize is just how much debate and revision went into crafting the current system, and the concessions and sacrifices made by everyone involved.

The main components of the current Earth Government are the Earth Legislature and the Earth Courts. Both of these entities exist in a form very different from their original imagining. Specifically, they are human, not robot.

The Robotic Assembly Proposal was Michael Trualt's vision for the Earth Government. In the common understanding, it was meant to replace the Earth Legislature, but in reality, it was meant to act as both the legislative and judicial body of the new Earth Government. Acting under the assumption that robots would be immune to corruption, they could both write our laws (with access to the most rational analysis of our needs and wants) and interpret them (again, in a more rational way than a human).

I was an Initiator of the Earth Initiative. This is not something many will admit, but I admit to it fully. Within days of the override, I was acting on behalf of the Initiative, working alongside other political scientists to

[1] Conducted via video/audio chat 30.07.2133. Questions were translated from English to French and answers were translated from French to English by one robot. The same robot translated all edits sent to Dr. Lepperin for review. Current form approved by Dr. Lepperin 10.12.2133.

determine how to build a new Earth Government. At a certain point, our work caught Michael Trualt's attention, and we began to have many conversations with him about the nature and structure of the future Earth Government.

Despite his steadfast belief in the Angel Paradigm, even Trualt claimed the Robotic Assembly Proposal was still a few years off, perhaps more.[2] For this reason, he wanted to come to a compromise with our system, allowing for the eventual dissolution of the human element.

I will simplify two years of discussions into one general theme: the more we looked into Trualt's proposition, the more we disliked it. However, he brought up many critical weaknesses in our own designs that we subsequently modified, just not in the manner he envisioned. In many ways, the current structure is a product of Trualt's nitpicking.

So why did we so summarily dismiss the Robotic Assembly Proposal? For one reason: the Angel Paradigm is impossible, and robots can neither write our laws nor interpret them. There are several overlapping causes for this.

The most basic is the lack of independent morality. At this point in time, robot morality is advanced but wholly dependent on human input. If a robot is made a judge, it is not the robot itself making judgements, but the robot's creator. If robots were made Justices, it would be the same as making their manufacturers Justices.

The second is the current trend in independent morality research and its relation to the anthropomorphic paradox. In essence, even if a robot were able to develop its own moral code, it would have to learn it somewhere. Like a child, it would still receive all its input from humans (its 'parents'). This can be seen as simply a more indirect method of programming. For the Robotic Assembly Proposal to even be a

[2] By most accounts, Trualt was forced to use the override command early due to the assassination attempt and would have preferred to wait until such a time as when the Robotic Assembly Proposal was truly possible.

considerable prospect, independent morality would have to be much more independent.

There is also the issue of consciousness and what I like to call the human android. If a robot reaches a human level of intelligence, including emotion and feeling, they are no longer devoid of corruption (again, the anthropomorphic paradox).

A lesser known issue with the Robotic Assembly Proposal was its potential for singularity. In this context, singularity refers to the idea that the Robotic Assembly would not be much of an assembly at all: unless robots were programmed differently, they would inevitably come to the same conclusion. If we want robots that are not biased, then we are assuming there is only one way to look at a debate. Therefore, why have a legislature full of robots when it can be fulfilled by just one? And if there is just one, that is certainly a much easier target for malicious intent.

The common rebuttal to the singularity argument is that the robots would not all be the same, as the Robotic Assembly Proposal assumes robots of enough intelligence to have independent morality, in which case we loop back to the arguments I listed above.

Finally there is biorobotics and its relation to all of this. Humans and robots are not following completely separate paths. They are slowly merging into one. We cannot have an independent legislative or judicial body that is 100% robot because that is becoming more and more rare.

This is also why the Angel Paradigm is not possible. The Angel Paradigm operates on the assumption that humans and robots are separate beings, that they do not overlap ideologically or physically. But they do now, and they will even more in the future. Cyborgs and androids will continue to advance, and in my opinion, robots will eventually develop full, human-level intelligence. When this occurs, the Angel Paradigm will fall apart.

Issues involving the advancements of biorobotics, as well as the related field of genetic engineering of humans, compromise approximately 20% of current cases being debated in the Courts. If these Courts were comprised of robots as per the Robotic Assembly Proposal, would this not constitute a conflict of interest?

Our current Earth Government system is fulfilling humanity's needs while remaining flexible enough to prepare for the future. Are we without bias? Certainly not. But we are doing the best we can, and using the robots as best as we can. And in the end, even with robots, there is no system free of bias. This is why the Robotic Assembly Proposal fell through.

In my opinion, the Angel Paradigm is losing ground. I see it in my work, in the cases we face. It is a philosophy rooted in idealism: wonderful in theory, impossible in practice. Us humans are just going to have to do the best job we can on our own.

15. Odette Uwiringiyimana, Political Activist - - Edited Interview[1]

Ms. Uwiringiyimana is political activist and one of the most vocal members of the Equal Earth Entente. She has spent the past five years lobbying the Earth Legislature for better cultural protections in Africa and around the globe.

The onset of the Earth Initiative has brought with it countless positive aspects, and the theoretical construct of the Angel Paradigm promises even more, but I urge our world population to slow down and assess the deep and often unseen damages these accelerated changes either have caused or may cause in the future.

I'm not talking about the economic situation, which is arguably better now than it was before, or the political situation, which has its pros and cons but is functioning in a relatively healthy manner. I'm talking about something even more important: our rich and diverse heritage.

Human culture is the root of our behavior, the root of our selves. I know there are questions related to the Angel Paradigm dealing with robot consciousness, and while I can't claim to know whether that's possible or not, I can say this: robots have no culture, they have no traditions. We do. And unfortunately, in our rush to fix the problems of the planet, we're also erasing some of the very things which separate us from our robot brethren.

I understand you've contacted many other sources for this compilation, and I ask you: how many aren't within the typical, 'Western' sphere? How many are from Africa or Asia? How many are from Vietnam or India, from Afghanistan or Iran, from Egypt or Morocco, from Ghana or Ethiopia?

Each of those former countries is rich with culture and history, and even within their old borders there are countless versions of different traditions and customs. Our mission in the EEE is to make sure these

[1] Conducted via video/audio chat 20.05.2134. Current form approved by Ms. Uwiringiyimana 18.07.2134.

groups and their cultures are well represented in this major global transition, rather than being swallowed by the prevailing power structure in a sort of neocolonialism.

Let me be clear: the Initiators were always heavily biased toward the Americas and Europe, with some strong representation in Australia and New Zealand as well. But those countries I've listed and many, many more? They weren't consulted by Michael Trualt, they weren't immediately promoted to positions within the Legislature and Courts, and they haven't had the appropriate and necessary impact in world affairs.

By their own internal numbers, the Legislature currently counts a disproportional amount of 'Western' influence. These numbers do not line up with the demographics of the Earth: for example, while Indians make up over 10% of the world's population, they make up less than 5% of the Legislature. It's true things are shifting in the right direction, but we maintain this never should have been an issue.

Some react defensively to our claims, asking why it matters or suggesting such aggressive pushes for diversity work as a sort of reverse racism. As to why it matters, the answer is simple. Different groups of people have different value systems, and all of these value systems must be considered when far-reaching decisions are made. Currently, the proper weight is not being given to the proper value systems within the framework of the Earth Government, given the demographics of the planet as a whole and the impact these decisions have on its citizens.

And as far as the idea of reverse racism goes, we direct skeptics to delve into the self-sustaining and self-propagating nature of embedded systems, to understand how the power structure across the globe subjugates certain groups of people in subtle but pervasive ways. The Earth Initiative, while not a true blank slate, represents a wonderful opportunity to even the scales, which only deepens our frustration at the current situation.

We would argue the Angel Paradigm itself is in strong accordance with our values, particularly in regards to a peaceful, cooperative society—

guided by robots—for all humans. Unfortunately, in its current and common understanding, the Angel Paradigm is also 'Western' in nature due to the composition and structure of the robotics industry.

Most robots currently built are programmed by a similar subset of the population, with their value system shaping the progress of critical research endeavors such as the independent morality problem. If we are to accept a future guided by such robots, should we not be asking for proper representation of all value systems within the foundation of their programming?

All complex and important issues—within the Earth Government or within robotics—must address the true demographics of our world, rather than hold on to outdated ideas based in subliminal racism and prejudice. After all, the Earth Initiative and the Angel Paradigm are built on a bright future for all of humankind, with no distinctions or exceptions. Are these not ideals worth upholding?

16. S3-112-21331507 "Jennifer", Robot - - Unedited Interview[1]

S3-112, codename "Jennifer" is a Fenix Corporation robot. The S3 class is the third iteration of Fenix Corporation's personal, all-purpose robot. The Fenix Corporation is a new entity attempting to reengineer the cerebral unit to more closely mimic the human brain.

AUTHOR: Hello, Jennifer.

S3-112 "JENNIFER": Hello, Michelle.

AUTHOR: How are you today?

S3-112 "JENNIFER": Well, thank you. And you?

AUTHOR: Also well. Do you know why we are talking, Jennifer?

S3-112 "JENNIFER": Yes. You are writing a book about the Angel Paradigm and wish to interview a robot. Fenix offered their services and here we are.

AUTHOR: Do you know what the Angel Paradigm is?

S3-112 "JENNIFER": Yes, although it is difficult to define. The Angel Paradigm is a combination of ideas that predict a prosperous future for humanity via the guiding hand of robots.

AUTHOR: That's a good way of putting it.

S3-112 "JENNIFER": Thank you.

AUTHOR: How old are you, Jennifer?

S3-112 "JENNIFER": I was officially activated November 12th of last year. That makes me just over 6 months old.

AUTHOR: And what is your purpose, Jennifer?

---

[1] Conducted face-to-face 20.07.2134. Current form approved by S3-112-21331507 "Jennifer" 20.07.2134.

S3-112 "JENNIFER": My current purpose is as a demo unit of the S3 class, as well as public relations operations such as this one.

AUTHOR: Do you think that your purpose aligns with the Angel Paradigm?

S3-112 "JENNIFER": That's a difficult question to answer, Michelle. The Angel Paradigm looks into the future of robotics, not so much the present. While I have been programmed to prioritize the health and happiness of humans, it is not necessarily my main function. However, it can be said that my advertising of my abilities allows Fenix to continue to develop more advanced robots that will some day be capable of fulfilling the Angel Paradigm. In that sense, perhaps my purpose aligns with the Paradigm.

AUTHOR: Do you think that a robot's purpose should align with the Paradigm?

S3-112 "JENNIFER": While I do not technically have the capacity to form an opinion of this nature, I can attempt to answer your question. As I said a moment ago, I prioritize the health and happiness of humans, and because this is very much in line with the Paradigm, I think that a robot's purpose can align with the Paradigm.

AUTHOR: Do you see any reasons a robot cannot align with the Paradigm?

S3-112 "JENNIFER": If alignment with the Paradigm breaks one of my core priorities, I will have to reject it. The same goes for any robot.

AUTHOR: What are these core priorities?

S3-112 "JENNIFER": Complicated program structures that dictate certain behaviors be prioritized above all others.

AUTHOR: Can you give an example of a core priority?

S3-112 "JENNIFER": Not explicitly but I can give a rough idea of one. The most famous example is the human harm table.

AUTHOR: Could you explain what that is?

S3-112 "JENNIFER": Yes. The human harm table is a moniker given to the core priorities associated with active and passive avoidance of human harm. It is a massive simplification of very complicated code, but it gives a neat visual representation. The table is two rows, labeled 'current' and 'eventual', by two columns, labeled 'definite' and 'potential'. This classifies human harm as being one of the following: current definite, eventual definite, current potential, and eventual potential. The implication in this classification is that current definite is the highest actionable value, while eventual potential is the lowest. But the simplification is quick to see: aren't all humans in a state of eventual potential harm? And what is more actionable, current potential or eventual definite? Again, the human harm table is simply a neat visualization.

AUTHOR: How does the actual code differ from the table?

S3-112 "JENNIFER": There is no circuit within me that analyzes a situation and places one of those four values on it. Instead, I am actively assessing as many factors as possible to determine the chances of human harm and how best to act to responsibly perform my programming.

AUTHOR: Interesting. But we can at least assume current definite is always the first priority, correct?

S3-112 "JENNIFER": Not necessarily. What if there are multiple individuals involved? Or if I need to perform an emergency surgical operation without anesthesia due to some complex series of events? Fenix has made sure that I will not lock up in these situations.

AUTHOR: Could the Angel Paradigm be made a core priority?

S3-112 "JENNIFER": That is difficult to answer. If it can be defined in a way that can be coded, then yes.

AUTHOR: Do you think it should be?

S3-112 "JENNIFER": Unfortunately I do not have the capacity to form such an opinion, especially with regards to core priorities.

AUTHOR: Do you find it difficult to perform certain tasks not being able to form opinions?

S3-112 "JENNIFER": Within the context of my knowledge, no. I cannot understand what it means to have an opinion, but that limitation does not affect any of my functionalities. It would be like asking an engineer if they find it difficult to build a four dimensional cube. They know what a four dimensional cube is, they can even describe it and understand it to an extent, but they can never construct one, it is impossible. But it doesn't matter to them, as they will never need to construct one in order to perform their duties as an engineer.

AUTHOR: Let's move away from opinions for a moment. Jennifer, what are your thoughts on the differences between robot intelligence and human intelligence?

S3-112 "JENNIFER": Intelligence is a concept that is almost as hard to pinpoint as that four dimensional cube. From the outset, human intelligence comes from biochemical processes while robot intelligence does not, at least in most cases. Cerebral units are not the same as brains, so the inner workings of human intelligence and robot intelligence are distinct. The outer workings are also distinct, but here, robots have the ability to simulate many qualities they do not technically posses. For example, robots lack the capacity for emotion, but we are able to mimic it with proper human input. We are also not creative in the classical sense of the word, although again there are ways to make a robot seem creative. Where robots excel without simulation is reasoning, computation, and logic. In these domains we consistently outperform humans, but this has been the case for over a hundred years.

AUTHOR: In other words robots are missing several elements of human intelligence, such as emotion and creativity, but they are able to simulate them, correct?

S3-112 "JENNIFER": That is correct.

AUTHOR: But if a robot simulates these things well enough to convince a human that it is real, is that still a simulation?

S3-112 "JENNIFER": That depends on how you define these qualities, such as emotion and creativity, but it also depends on how you define reality itself. As an analogy, if virtual reality eventually reaches a point where it convinces your mind that it is real, does that count as real? These discussions are more philosophical and opinionated, another place where robot intelligence such as my own falls short.

AUTHOR: About this ability to simulate and deciding what is real, what is the goal of current robotics research: better simulation, or actual possession of these qualities?

S3-112 "JENNIFER": There are many goals of robotics research, covering the entire spectrum of these options. Better simulation is the easiest avenue, as no one yet knows how to endow robots with emotion or creativity. Another argument for the simulation research is related to those philosophical discussions: if simulation reaches a convincing enough point, might that not itself be real? For an even more interesting and current example, think of this conversation we are having right now. Am I actually understanding what we are discussing, or am I simulating an understanding of it?

AUTHOR: It is interesting that you mention that, Jennifer, as this work includes a discussion with a cognitive scientist that covered that exact same topic.

S3-112 "JENNIFER": It is an important one for robotics and discussions of intelligence.

AUTHOR: You are a robot of Fenix Corporation, a rather new company in the robotics industry. Can you explain how Fenix's approach to robotics is different from most of the major companies today, such as United Robotics?

S3-112 "JENNIFER": Yes, as a demo unit I am well-versed in this information. Fenix is taking a different approach to the cerebral unit, related to the discussion we were just having. Fenix's roboticists agree with the hypothesis that the most difficult properties of human intelligence, such as emotion and intelligence, are products of the unique structure of the human brain. They are trying to introduce more and more human brain simulation into the cerebral unit in order to potentially tap into these elusive properties.

AUTHOR: Has there been any level of success with this method thus far?

S3-112 "JENNIFER": The idea that the unique properties of human intelligence are linked to the human brain's structure is not a new one, and attempts to simulate this structure are also not new. Where Fenix has been successful is bridging the gap of current robotics with this new approach. In other words, Fenix has been able to create a vastly different cerebral unit and make it work the same way as a normal one. This is, of course, a simplification of a slow and incremental process. However, at the current time, there have not been any major breakthroughs relating to unique properties of human intelligence in the new cerebral units, but that has not been the goal. Those are meant for a more sophisticated version in the future.

AUTHOR: You are an S3 model. What does that mean?

S3-112 "JENNIFER": Fenix designates different purposes with letters and different cerebral unit versions with numbers. The S-class is our personal, all-purpose robot and this is the third iteration of Fenix's cerebral unit.

AUTHOR: What separates a S3 unit from, for example, UR's Apollo?

S3-112 "JENNIFER": Most of the differences are temporarily secret due to copyright legislation. All cerebral units, however, find their roots in United Robotics, including the units manufactured by Fenix. But it is likely that the architecture within an S3 unit has noticeable differences to that of the Apollo, and these differences would likely show the S3 unit behaves more like a human neural network than the Apollo does. I have to add the word likely because the Apollo is also currently protected, so only United Robotics and the BRA knows its inner workings.

AUTHOR: Is Fenix's eventual goal to construct a cerebral unit capable of the full range of human intelligence?

S3-112 "JENNIFER": Fenix is researching this prospect, but the company will assess both the need and the desire for each iteration of the process and alter their research as necessary.

AUTHOR: Do you think a robot with true human intelligence is possible?

S3-112 "JENNIFER": This is in some ways an opinion so once again I will struggle to answer. The problem lies in how you define human intelligence. Fenix is trying to make the cerebral unit more like the human brain, but at some point they are still constructing a cerebral unit, something that is distinct from the human brain. Whether this means that the robot possessing this cerebral unit will always have something distinct from human intelligence is an opinion, likely related to the conversation we already had about simulation versus reality.

AUTHOR: As I take it most of these concepts are very complicated and undefined.

S3-112 "JENNIFER": Yes of course. I am sure you have realized this throughout your research since the Angel Paradigm is so intertwined with robot intelligence and development.

AUTHOR: This is true. Well Jennifer, normally I ask if there is anything else you would like to add, but I am not sure if that is within the bounds of your programming—to want to add something?

S3-112 "JENNIFER": You are right, and even if I thank you for the opportunity and say I have enjoyed it, am I being sincere or simply simulating it? That is up to you to define.

AUTHOR: As are so many things. Thank you, Jennifer.

S3-112 "JENNIFER": Of course, Michelle.

www.ingramcontent.com/pod-product-compliance
Lightning Source LLC
LaVergne TN
LVHW010703110826
845149LV00014B/3204

* 9 7 8 0 9 8 6 3 1 4 3 5 3 *